A MOST UNUSUAL GOVERNESS

A MOST UNUSUAL GOVERNESS

Amanda Grange

Chivers Press
Bath, England
•
Thorndike Press
Waterville, Maine USA

This Large Print edition is published by Chivers Press, England, and by Thorndike Press, USA.

Published in 2002 in the U.K. by arrangement with Robert Hale Ltd.

Published in 2002 in the U.S. by arrangement with Robert Hale Ltd.

U.K. Hardcover ISBN 0–7540–4813–6 (Chivers Large Print)
U.K. Softcover ISBN 0–7540–4814–4 (Camden Large Print)
U.S. Softcover ISBN 0–7862–3959–X (General Series Edition)

The text of this Large Print edition is unabridged.
Other aspects of the book may vary from the original edition.

Set in 16 pt. New Times Roman.

Printed in Great Britain on acid-free paper.

British Library Cataloguing in Publication Data available

Library of Congress Cataloging-in-Publication Data

Grange, Amanda.
A most unusual governess / Amanda Grange.
p. cm.
ISBN 0–7862–3959–X (lg. print : sc : alk. paper)
1. Governesses—Fiction. 2. England—Fiction. 3. Large type books. I. Title.
PR6107.R35 M68 2002
823'.92—dc21 2001059121

CHAPTER ONE

'Out with it, Constance!'

Lady Constance Templeton, startled out of her reverie, almost dropped her porcelain teacup in surprise. 'Really, Isabelle!' she retorted, once she had recovered herself. 'I don't know what you mean.'

The two ladies, both vigorous despite being over seventy years of age, were taking tea in the splendid drawing-room of Templeton House. It was a hot afternoon in the summer of 1814, and the tall windows were open to let in the cooling breeze.

'How long have we known each other?' demanded Isabelle, fixing her friend with a shrewd eye.

'I don't see what that has to do with anything,' returned Lady Constance evasively.

'Oh, don't you?' snorted Isabelle. She put down her cup with a determined clatter. 'We have been friends for the best part of fifty years, Constance, and I know instinctively when something is wrong. And something is wrong now. No, don't bother denying it,' she said, with a firm shake of her head. 'I won't be put off. And I won't rest until I know what it is. Although, from the way your eyes keep drifting to the portrait of your nephew, I can guess. It is my belief it has something to do with James.'

As she spoke, her own eyes turned to the large portrait that hung above the magnificent Adam fireplace. It was of a strikingly handsome young man, with black hair and coal-black eyes. High cheekbones and a determined chin defined his face, in the same way that long, firm limbs and a broad chest defined his body. Strong hands held the reins of the stallion he was riding, and although the animal was rearing he controlled it with an air of arrogant ease.

'Arrogance,' said Isabelle, as she continued to look at the portrait, not realizing she had spoken out loud.

Lady Constance gave a heavy sigh. 'Arrogance,' she agreed. 'Pride, pigheadedness and downright stubbornness! Why he doesn't see what he is doing to the children is beyond me.'

'Aha!' said Isabelle triumphantly. 'I knew there was something.' She picked up her chicken-skin fan and wafted it in front of her bony chest. 'What has James been doing to make you so distracted this time?'

Lady Constance shook her grey head with vexation. 'It is too bad, Isabelle, it really is. Especially after the last time. He has scared yet another governess away.'

'Another one? But Miss Raistrick only left six weeks ago! Miss Farthingale hasn't had time to be scared away.'

'Miss Farthingale!' exclaimed Lady Constance, raising her thin eyebrows. 'My dear Isabelle, you are behind the times. Miss Farthingale lasted only two days! Which is a great pity, as she spoke not only fluent French and German but Russian besides. No, it is not Miss Farthingale this time, it is Miss Dove who has packed her bags and, like her namesake, flown away!'

'But what is the reason for it?' enquired Isabelle with a frown.

'My dear Isabelle, what is always the reason? Discipline.'

'A very good thing,' said Isabelle stoutly.

'Of course it is, in moderation. But James doesn't seem to have realized he is no longer in the army. It is discipline, discipline, discipline, morning, noon and night. He treats his estate as though it is a parade ground, and he treats the children like raw recruits. Do you know, Isabelle, he never allows the children to play, but has them marching along the terrace twice a day instead? And when poor Miss Farthingale tried to protest, he had *her* marching along the terrace as well!'

'But why did she not stand up to him?' demanded Isabelle. She folded her fan with a snap. 'Why did she not tell him that it would not do?'

'Have you ever tried standing up to James?' asked Lady Constance quellingly.

Isabelle remembered the last time she had

encountered James—Lord Randall—and pursed her lips. At six feet two inches tall and thirty-five years of age, he was not an easy man to stand up to. Particularly as his height and maturity were matched by a commanding presence—the result of ten years spent fighting in the army against Napoleon—and a formidable will.

'I *see.*'

'Really, Isabelle, I don't know *what* to do. Given time he will adjust to civilian life, but he has seen so little of the children whilst he has been abroad that he has lost touch with their needs.'

'It is such a pity their parents were killed,' sighed Isabelle.

'It is. But James is a loving uncle and a caring guardian. It is just that, at the moment, being so newly returned from the army, he is too strict. I have managed to persuade him to let Lucilla come to me for a few weeks.' Lady Constance's face softened as she thought of her great-niece who, at six years old, was adorable. 'But he will not let me have the boys as well. He is concerned to make sure they don't fall behind with their studies, particularly as he promised their mother, on her deathbed, that he would not send them away to school. They are too busy to come to me, he said—'

'But Preston can't be more than ten years old!' interrupted Isabelle. 'And Fitzwilliam is only eleven. Studies are all very well in their place, but in all this heat? Constance, you must do something. You must take a hand. At least until James has adjusted to the children. They require a new governess, you say? Very well, you must appoint the young lady yourself. Some sensible person who will be sensitive to their needs, and who will stand no nonsense from James.'

'Even if I could, by some miracle, find someone like that, it would not answer, because James has forbidden me to interfere. He is quite capable of appointing his own staff, he told me—in no uncertain terms.' She leaned back on the sofa, and for the first time her full age became apparent. There was a tired set to her shoulders, and there were deep lines around her eyes. 'Besides, at the moment I have problems of my own.'

'Ah! Yes. I had forgotten. Your knees. Poor Constance: it is a trial to grow old.' She continued on a brighter note. 'Have you had any luck in finding a companion yet? Any answers to your advertisement? I must say I think it is a good idea. Having someone to fetch and carry for you will save a great deal of wear and tear on your legs—one doesn't always want to be asking the servants.'

'I am beginning to think it is impossible to find anyone who will suit.' Lady Constance's eye fell on the beautifully chased silver teapot that stood on the low table next to the sofa. 'More tea, Isabelle?' she enquired.

'Thank you, Constance, I will.'

Lady Constance filled both cups with the clear, fragrant liquid and together the two ladies enjoyed the refreshing drink.

'To answer your question,' Lady Constance continued when her cup was once again empty, 'no, I haven't found a companion—at least, not yet. I have seen three ladies so far, and they have all been impossible. One of them was even older than me!'

'Oh, Constance, that would never do! Have you anyone left?'

Lady Constance sighed. 'I'm seeing Miss Rodgers tomorrow, and Miss Davenport this afternoon. I only hope one of them will do.'

There was a whirring sound. The long-case clock in the corner was preparing to strike the hour.

'Good gracious!' exclaimed Isabelle as the first chime reverberated through the room. 'Is that the time? I must go. Edward is taking me to Mrs Skeffington's this evening, and it will take me an age to dress.' She stood up in a rustle of silk. 'You must come to me on Thursday and let me know how you get on.'

'I will.' Lady Constance, rising, did not sound hopeful.

Isabelle kissed her friend on the cheek. 'You will find someone, Constance, I'm sure of it.' She took her friend's hands and gave them an affectionate squeeze. 'Miss Davenport may be just what you need.'

*   *   *

Sarah Davenport was at that moment waiting in the hall below. The butler had left her alone whilst he went to enquire whether Lady Templeton was ready to receive her, and she was making the most of the opportunity to tidy herself in front of one of the hall's gilded mirrors. Her auburn hair was arranged neatly in a bun, but one or two tendrils had fallen loose. She tucked them in, securing them with a pin, then turned her attention to her yellow muslin gown. It had grown limp with the heat, but otherwise was not too shabby. She puffed out the short sleeves and adjusted the buckle that trimmed the high waist, then arranged her reticule so that its barest patches were hidden. Having checked her appearance, she began to walk around the hall.

She was not looking forward to the coming interview. She never liked interviews, but in her present circumstances they were a necessary evil and she wished this one would begin. She was trying to take her mind off things by admiring the gilded furniture when, to her surprise, a little girl of about six years of age came into view.

Sarah smiled and felt her tension dissolve. The little girl was as pretty as a picture, with golden hair curled into ringlets and large blue eyes. She was exquisitely dressed, her silk frock and frilled pantaloons coming straight from the pages of *Ackermann's Repository*; one of Sarah's favourite journals in happier days.

'Hello.' Sarah's greeting was friendly.

The little girl did not reply. Instead she stayed at the far side of the hall, looking at Sarah uncertainly. Sarah was about to speak again when she noticed that the little girl's forearm was grazed.

'You've hurt yourself,' she said, going forward to look more closely. 'How did it happen? Did you fall?'

Again the little girl did not reply.

Thinking she must be unusually shy, Sarah said, 'Well, run along then, dear, and show your mama. She'll soon make it better for you.'

The little girl, whilst never taking her eyes off Sarah, stood on one pantalooned leg. Lifting the other leg behind her she held it there with one hand. Then, balancing precariously, she said, 'I don't have a mama. My mama is dead.'

Sarah now understood the cause of the little girl's withdrawn nature. 'I'm sorry to hear that,' she said gently. 'Run along, then, and show your nurse, my dear. I'm sure she will be wondering where you are.'

The little girl put down her leg and lifted the other one. Slowly she shook her head.

'Don't you want to?' asked Sarah.

She was beginning to sense that, underneath the silk dress and frilled pantaloons, the little girl was not very happy.

The child again shook her head. Then, by way of explanation, she said, 'Nurse will be cross.'

She had taken Sarah's measure and had decided to trust her.

Sarah smiled reassuringly. 'I'm sure she won't. But the graze does need cleaning. Look, it's all dirty and there are some pieces of grit that need washing out. Run along and show your nurse. She'll wash it for you, and then you'll be as good as new.'

Once more the little girl shook her head.

'Why do you think your nurse will be cross?' asked Sarah with a frown. She had dismissed the idea at first, but the little girl seemed convinced and Sarah realized she would not be able to persuade her to return to her nurse until the problem had been sorted out.

'Because,' said the little girl with an air of finality.

Then, a minute later she decided to elaborate. 'Because I was playing.' She hesitated and then confided, 'I'm not allowed to play.'

Sarah was startled. 'Not allowed to play? *All* children should be allowed to play. Well . . .' Her voice tailed off as she realized she did not know the little girl's name. She lifted her eyebrows. 'Do you have a name?' she asked.

The tiniest smile broke out at the corner of the child's mouth. 'It's Lucilla,' she said, adding with a gurgle, '*Every*one has a name'

Sarah laughed. 'Well, Lucilla—or may I call you Lucy?' Lucy nodded. 'Well, then, Lucy, if your nurse will be cross with you for playing I suggest we mend matters ourselves. Show me your arm.'

Lucy hesitated and then, putting down her leg, she held her grazed arm out to Sarah.

Sarah examined the graze. 'That doesn't seem too bad. I think we can manage without troubling anyone else. Now,' she went on, taking a clean linen handkerchief out of her threadbare reticule, 'spit!'

Lucy's eyes widened in horror.

'It's quite all right,' Sarah reassured her. 'Just this once. When you've spat on the handkerchief I can use it to clean your arm.'

Lucy hesitated and then, summoning all her courage, she did as she was asked.

'Good girl.' Sarah smiled, then formed the handkerchief into a tighter pad and used the moistened linen to dab Lucy's arm. She cleaned the graze slowly and carefully and was rewarded by the little girl's patience. 'There.' She let go of Lucy's arm. 'It's as good as new. No one needs to know what happened. And now . . .' she went on, standing up. But before she could continue, she heard footsteps: Warner, Lady Templeton's butler, was returning.

With one last glance at Sarah, Lucy disappeared down one of the corridors which led off from the hall, leaving Sarah to face the butler alone.

He fixed her with a disapproving eye. In his opinion, young ladies who had applied for a position as a companion shouldn't forget their station in life by talking freely to members of the family, however young those members might be.

Ignoring his disapproval, Sarah folded her handkerchief and tucked it away in her shabby reticule.

'Her ladyship will see you now,' the butler informed her majestically. 'Be so good as to follow me.'

*   *   *

'Come in, Miss Davenport. Do sit down.'

Lady Templeton waved an elegant hand towards a chair that had been arranged on the other side of her rosewood desk.

Sarah dutifully sat down, and Lady Templeton continued. 'I think we will begin by discussing your background, and then you may tell me why you decided to apply for a position as my companion.'

Lady Templeton assumed an expression of interest as Sarah began, but in fact she scarcely listened to what Sarah was saying. She was too busy recalling the scene she had witnessed in the hall a few minutes before, which she had happened upon quite by chance as she had been *en route* from the drawing-room to the office where she interviewed her staff. She had seen Sarah's meeting with Lucy, and had overheard almost all of their conversation. Her anger at discovering that even Lucy's nurse—no doubt following James's orders—would not allow the little girl to play had gradually subsided, and what she had then seen and heard had given her pause for thought. She had realized at once that Miss Davenport was too young to be a suitable companion for her. She felt a twinge of guilt that she had not said so at once, but she dismissed it by telling herself that perhaps she might be able to offer Miss Davenport another position. The young lady before her had a rapport with children, and that rapport had set Lady Templeton to wondering whether she dare defy her nephew and appoint Lucy's new governess herself.

But as Sarah finished speaking she dismissed the idea with a reluctant sigh.

Miss Davenport might have a rapport with children, but there was no reason to suppose she would be able to stand up to James, any more than the long line of governesses who had passed through the doors of Watermead Grange.

'Thank you, Miss Davenport. Most clear. Unfortunately, I don't think this is the right position for you.'

She stretched out her hand for the silver bell that sat on the edge of her desk.

'May I ask why not?' enquired Sarah.

Lady Templeton's eyebrows rose; it was the first time she had ever had one of her decisions questioned. 'Since you ask, you are too young to be a suitable companion for me. From your letter'—here she picked up the letter which was lying on her desk—'I'd gained the impression you were older. I'm sorry to disappoint you, but the fact of the matter is that I need a mature woman. Unfortunately, you're not suitable for the position.'

Sarah listened to this speech with a mixture of surprise and disappointment. But she had a strong character and would not be so easily deterred; particularly as her small savings had dwindled into almost nothing, and her situation was verging on the desperate. 'I am not as young as I look, and my experiences have matured me beyond my years. I am used to being with older people. As I told you, I spent many years nursing my mother before she died. I believe you wouldn't be disappointed if you took me on.'

Lady Templeton's surprise deepened. She was not used to being argued with. Particularly not by someone applying for a position as her companion.

Ordinarily, it would have irritated her. But now it made her wonder whether she *should* choose a governess for the children herself. A young lady who could stand up to *her* may also be able to stand up to James . . .

But no. Miss Davenport, having made her protest, would most probably fall at the next obstacle.

'You don't lack spirit,' Lady Templeton acknowledged. 'But you cannot be more than twenty-one or two, whereas I am looking for a companion who is nearer fifty years of age.'

'Then perhaps, if age was so important to you, it would have been as well to say so in the advertisement. I have had a long journey on hot and dusty roads; something I could have been spared if you had given a little more thought to your requirements.'

Lady Templeton's hand crept back from the silver bell. 'You interest me, Miss Davenport,' she said. 'Are you always so outspoken?'

Sarah's face fell as she realized that her tongue had run away with her. She gave a rueful smile. 'My father called it my besetting sin,' she admitted.

'I think, in this case,' said Lady Templeton thoughtfully, 'it might just be a virtue. Tell me, Miss Davenport, have you ever thought of becoming a governess?'

Sarah shook her head. 'My accomplishments aren't good enough. My painting is poor, I am an indifferent pianist, and I never *could* master the harp!'

Lady Templeton felt a touch of sympathy; she, too, had never been able to master the instrument! But, in this instance, playing the harp was unimportant. She fixed Sarah with a clear eye. 'Do you really believe that children should be allowed to play?' she shot out.

Sarah was startled. She had had no idea that her conversation with Lucy had been overheard. 'How did you . . .?'

'I was on the landing,' said Lady Templeton. 'I could not help but overhear.' She paused. 'What did you think of my great-niece?'

Sarah hesitated. 'She's beautiful.'

'But?' enquired Lady Templeton. There had been a definite 'but' hanging unspoken in the air.

Sarah sighed. 'But I don't think she's very happy. Golden curls and silk dresses are all very well in their way . . .'

'Go on.'

'But little girls aren't dolls. They need to know how to behave, of course, but they need to have fun as well, and they can't do that if they are never allowed to play.'

Lady Templeton gave a thoughtful nod. Then, coming to a decision, she determined to risk James's wrath. Lucy needed a new governess, and even if Miss Davenport turned out to be no better than the others, she could hardly be any worse.

'Miss Davenport,' she said, 'I have a suggestion to make . . .'

* * *

Sarah looked around the schoolroom as she

sat at her desk marking an assortment of exercises. Little had she guessed, when she had gone to Templeton House not three weeks before, that instead of ending up as a companion she would end up as a governess.

Her first few weeks at Watermead Grange, Lord Randall's estate in the county of Kent, had passed both quickly and enjoyably. Despite Lady Templeton's warnings that Lord Randall was not an easy man to work for, and despite her declaration that he had scared away all the previous governesses—including poor Miss Farthingale, who had left after only two days!—Sarah had settled in well; although, as Lord Randall was absent, this was perhaps not as encouraging as it seemed. The true test would come when he returned.

The schoolroom was large and airy. It was situated at the top of the house, with a window to the west. It was clean, and was well furnished with everything she could need, including desks, chairs, globes and maps. Lord Randall may be a difficult man to work for, but at least he provided well.

The children had turned out to be delightful. As well as Lucy there were also Lucy's two older brothers, Fitzwilliam and Preston, whom Sarah looked after in the evenings when their tutors had left the Grange. True, Fitzwilliam had been pale and withdrawn when she had first arrived, whilst Preston had been restless with suppressed energy. But a few weeks of running around after lessons had finished, and of playing ordinary childhood games, had soon changed the children for the better and Sarah was pleased to see just how happy and confident they had become.

She was just about to dip her quill into the ink-pot on her desk when she heard the sound of someone running up the corridor. A moment later Edna, one of the housemaids, burst into the room.

'Beggin' your pardon, miss, for bursting in like this, but I've so much to do,' said Edna, who was red in the face and obviously flustered. 'The missus says . . . Mrs Smith . . . that is to say, the housekeeper, miss . . . she sent me to tell you . . .'

'Tell me what?' asked Sarah, mystified, as Edna caught her breath.

'It's the master, miss. Lord Randall. He'll be home by the end of the week!'

CHAPTER TWO

'Welcome home, my lord,' said Hodgess, the butler, as Lord Randall strode into the house with all the unthinking arrogance of a rich and powerful man.

'Thank you, Hodgess.' Lord Randall looked round him as though he was pleased to be home.

He was still recognizably the man in the portrait hanging in Lady Templeton's drawing-room. Although the portrait had been painted in 1804, the intervening ten years had changed him very little. He had the same proud features, the same black hair and the same black eyes, only now they had the look of seasoned maturity instead of the look of untried youth.

His figure, too, had changed very little. Whilst many of his fellows had gone to seed, Lord Randall had retained the firm and powerful body of his early years. The time he had spent serving with Wellington in the war against Napoleon had defined his muscles, hardening them, and giving him the sleek and powerful look of a jungle cat.

'You had a good journey, I hope?' murmured Hodgess deferentially, taking Lord Randall's tall hat.

'Yes, thank you.' Lord Randall's glance around the hall had now become more focused, and he was taking in every inch of the magnificent entrance. 'I see the worn baluster has been replaced,' he said, his eyes coming to rest on the sweeping staircase.

'Yes, my lord,' said Hodgess. 'As you instructed.'

'And the panelling in the library?'

'Yes, my lord.'

'Good. The light's fading now but I'll

inspect it in the morning, before I ride round the estate. Tell Dawson I'll want him tomorrow, and most probably on Friday as well. I want to get the estate business out of the way as quickly as possible—before the preparations for the house-party begin.'

'Very good, my lord.'

Hodgess, together with the rest of the staff, had been thrown into a flurry of activity when the message had arrived that not only would Lord Randall shortly be paying a visit to the estate, but that he would also be organizing a house-party. Which meant that his visit would be much longer than usual.

'And by the way, Hodgess,' said Lord Randall as he picked up the post which had been laid in readiness for him on a silver salver—including, on the bottom of the pile, a letter from his aunt—there will be two guests arriving later this evening: my cousin, Mr Shuttleworth, and his travelling companion, Mrs de Bracy. They're attending a wedding in Sussex and will be breaking their journey here. They will stay tonight and tomorrow night, and will leave on Friday.'

'Very good, my lord,' said Hodgess—the phrase which accounted for most of his dealings with his lord and master!—'I will see that Mrs Smith is informed.'

'Mrs de Bracy will have the Elizabethan suite,' went on Lord Randall, 'and Mr Shuttleworth will have one of the rooms in the bachelor wing. See to it, Hodgess, if you please.'

'At once my lord,' said Hodgess. He made a low bow and withdrew.

Lord Randall glanced once more around the hall, then, still sorting through his post, he began to climb the stairs.

* * *

Sarah was in her room, reading. She was stretched out on the window-seat with the mullioned window wide open next to her so that she could make the most of the cool evening air. The day had been hot and she welcomed the breeze that had sprung up.

Her room, a large and spacious apartment, was at the back of the house. For all that, it was very pleasant, and overlooked the rose gardens. It was far better than anything she had been expecting, and its loveliness had taken her by surprise. She had soon learnt from the servants, however, that although Lord Randall was a hard taskmaster he always treated his staff well. There were no damp attics or rat-infested servants' quarters at Watermead Grange as there were in many other great houses; everything was neat, clean and well ordered. The lower servants—scullery-maids, kitchen-maids and the like—slept in clean, dry, attic rooms, and the higher servants—butler and housekeeper—together with the governess, were all housed on the second floor, in rooms that were almost good enough for guests.

Sarah's eyes roamed round the room. The heavy four-poster bed, with its green silk drapes and its pile of soft pillows, was something she had loved on sight. Beyond it was a carved oak wardrobe, an inlaid writing-desk and a large oak chest, as well as two chairs—one a padded armchair covered in a deep-green damask, and the other an elegant, upright Hepplewhite chair—which flanked the fireplace. And in the furthest corner of the room was an ornate washstand.

Her eyes lingered on the washstand. It was late in the evening and she felt hot and sticky. She crossed the room, and was about to pour some water from the delicate porcelain ewer into the flower-painted bowl when she had a better idea. She would take a turn around the garden in order to really feel the benefit of the cooling breeze. Then she would turn in for the night.

She went out on to the landing and down the stairs, but just as she reached the first turning she heard someone coming up from below. A moment later, Lord Randall came into view.

Sarah knew a brief moment of panic before her customary good sense reasserted itself. She had not expected to meet Lord Randall on the stairs but she would have to meet him at some time; she might as well get it over with! She had just time to smooth her hands over her skirt and push a stray tendril of hair back behind her ears before Lord Randall looked up and saw her.

Her heart missed a beat: his dark good looks took her by surprise. His face was arresting—the high cheekbones, straight nose and decided chin gave it strength, whilst his eyes, black like his hair, gave it character—and his body was lean and powerful.

Instead of greeting her, however, as she had expected, a look of irritation crossed his face. His eyes flicked over her, taking her in from head to foot: the auburn hair, the oval face, the sea-green eyes, the clear skin; and the slight but subtly curved figure.

Then his eyes flicked back to her own. 'The front stairs are not for the use of housemaids,' he said briefly. 'The back stairs are for your use.'

Sarah was taken aback.

'I don't know what liberties you've been taking in my absence, but you won't take them again. Return to your own part of the house at once,' he said arrogantly. 'And tell Mrs Smith I don't expect to see any of the housemaids out of uniform again.'

Realizing that she must correct his mistake, Sarah said, 'I am not a housemaid. I'm Miss Davenport, the new governess.' She gave him her brightest smile and held out her hand for him to shake.

'I haven't appointed a governess,' he said, looking her up and down once more before beginning to mount the next stair.

Sarah dropped her hand in surprise. She had expected him to know all about her appointment. 'I was appointed by Lady Templeton.'

He paused, frowning.

'I took up my appointment three weeks ago,' Sarah went on, 'and I've been teaching Lucy—Lucilla,' she corrected herself—'since I arrived.'

'Lady Templeton doesn't have the authority to appoint my staff,' he remarked.

Sarah's eyes widened. She had been prepared for arrogance, but not this! She stood her ground, however, saying, 'Nevertheless, she appointed me.'

He raised his eyebrows. 'I find that difficult to believe.'

'Are you doubting my word?' She forgot for a moment that she was a mere governess and the question came out as a direct challenge.

But instead of taking up her challenge he ignored it altogether, and she realized that he considered her questions to be beneath his notice.

She was beginning to understand why the other governesses had run away!

'What are your qualifications?' he asked her suddenly. The hand holding his letters had dropped to his side and it seemed he meant to give her his attention. 'I take it you are a musician, but what instruments do you play besides the piano and the harp?' He went on immediately, without giving her time to reply. 'Do you speak French and Italian? Can you paint and sketch? Can you instruct Lucilla in the use of maps and globes?' He was feeling annoyed that his aunt had appointed a governess behind his back, but even so, he had to admit that if Miss Davenport was suitable it would save him a lot of trouble. Appointing governesses had never been one of his favourite occupations!

'I don't know anyone with so many accomplishments,' said Sarah in astonishment, when at last he gave her a moment to speak. 'If those are your requirements I'm surprised you've ever managed to find anyone at all.'

'Every governess at Watermead Grange has met those requirements,' he told her. 'Miss Farthingale also spoke Russian and German.'

'Then it's a pity she only stayed two days,' Sarah returned.

He looked at her curiously, but her face gave him no clue as to what she was thinking. And after wondering fleetingly whether she was being impertinent, he rejected the idea. A governess, being impertinent to Lord Randall? Of course not!

'Indeed,' he said; but still, there was a hint of puzzlement on his face: somehow, the conversation didn't seem to be going as he had expected. But then he banished his puzzlement, and made an efrort to put the conversation back on more normal lines. 'Let us hope you fare better than she did. In the meantime, you will join me in my study at eight o'clock tomorrow morning and show me some of Lucilla's work. I'll want your opinion of her capabilities as well as—'

'Her *capabilities*?' Sarah's eyes flashed as her astonishment at this speech gave way to anger; she could not believe that he was talking about dear little Lucy in such a cold-blooded manner. 'Lucy is only six years—'

'I have had a long journey, Miss Davenport,' he interrupted her wearily, 'and I don't intend to waste the rest of my evening in conversation with a governess.'

And so saying he walked past her, overtopping her by a good eight inches as he reached the same stair, before mounting to the landing and disappearing from view.

Almost taking Sarah's breath away. The arrogance! she thought. The overbearing, overweening conceit of the man!

I don't intend to waste the rest of my evening in conversation with a governess indeed.

But as she began to recover from the encounter she had to acknowledge that she had been warned. 'He is arrogant, high-handed and overbearing,' Lady Templeton had said.

Yes. He was certainly that.

But he was also, she realized unwillingly, the most attractive man she had ever seen. It wasn't only anger that had set her heart racing as she had confronted him, it was some deeper feminine instinct; an instinct which, until that moment, she had not known she possessed.

She took a firm hold of herself. Lord Randall was undeniably attractive, but he was also her extremely arrogant employer, and instead of dwelling on his powerful body and broodingly handsome face she needed to think about the coming interview, and decide what she was going to say.

Because of one thing she was sure: no matter how much she needed the position she did not intend to be used as a doormat. If Lord Randall thought he could walk all over her, then Lord Randall must think again!

* * *

'*There* you are, James!' said Maud de Bracy later that evening, as Lord Randall finally walked into the drawing-room. 'I was beginning to think you had forgotten me!'

'And me,' added Percy Shuttleworth, from his place on the piano-stool. Percy had a habit of fiddling with the keys of the pianoforte whenever he was bored, and his tuneless ditties had made more than one host wish they had never purchased an instrument.

'*Every*one forgets you, Percy,' remarked

Maud, getting up from the elegant settee and going over to James.

'I had business to attend to,' said James.

'Business!' exclaimed Maud. 'You've only been in the house a few hours! What business could you possibly have?'

'An estate the size of Watermead doesn't run itself,' he said with a smile.

'It always seems to,' remarked Percy, his hands thrust deep into his well-cut pockets. He half-turned on the stool to face James, one foot resting on the fine Aubusson carpet whilst the other dangled above it. 'Whenever I'm here it's always the same: Hodgess appearing and disappearing like the genie of the lamp, making sure that everything is just as it ought to be. This house runs so perfectly it must be magic! And the grounds,' he continued, glancing out of the tall windows. 'The grounds here are always amazing. Even the trees seem to grow straighter at Watermead than anywhere else! The whole thing is perfect; there's never a blade of grass out of place!'

'The grass wouldn't *dare* be out of place. Would it, James?' Maud asked archly, taking his arm and looking up into his face. 'But tell me,' she went on, seeing that he was not in the mood to be teased. 'How was your journey, James?'

'Hot and dusty,' he remarked with a wry smile. He sat down in an elegant Hepplewhite chair.

'Ours was exactly the same,' said Percy.

'Terrible,' agreed Maud. 'It's a wonder I'm not a wreck.'

'You? A wreck?' laughed Percy. 'You always look magnificent. Doesn't she, Randall?'

James ran his eye over Maud de Bracy: the luxurious dark hair, the skilfully painted face, the scarlet satin gown—just a little too low-cut—and the hard eyes. 'Magnificent? Yes.' He nodded slowly. 'You could say that.'

Percy laughed. 'Which is as near to a compliment as you will ever get from James.'

'Compliments are for the weak-minded,' James remarked ironically.

'Which puts you in a devil of a pickle, Maud,' said Percy. 'You either have to admit you like compliments and resign yourself to being classed as weak-minded, or else pretend you don't like them and never hear another one again!'

'I didn't come here for the compliments,' shrugged Maud. Nevertheless she looked displeased. 'Besides, James's time for paying compliments to other women will soon be over. Or, at least, I think it will. Put me out of my misery, James, and tell me: have you offered for Margaret Leatherhead yet?'

He shook his head. 'Not yet.'

'So you mean to ask her at the house-party,' said Maud.

'Yes.'

'Don't know what you see in the girl,'

remarked Percy.

James shrugged. 'She comes from a good family and she's been gently bred. She's meek, respectful, quiet and biddable—everything a wife should be, in fact.'

If Percy thought that James was about to make the same mistake twice he did not have the courage to say so. Instead he said, 'Can't think what you're marrying for anyway. You've got two nephews. It's not as if you need an heir.'

'But I do need someone to protect me from every miss who fancies herself a countess, and every matchmaking mama!'

Percy laughed. 'Being hunted, James? One of the perils of being an earl.'

'But one that will disappear when I marry again.'

'And what about the children?' asked Percy. 'There's a lot more to being your wife than just having you as a husband. Does Margaret know what she'll be taking on?'

'The children will be cared for by their nurse, their tutors and their governess—'

'So you've found a replacement,' Percy interrupted. 'Let's hope this one's better than the last one! Poor Miss Dove quaked every time you so much as looked at her!'

'Miss Davenport doesn't quake,' said James. His thoughts went to the determined figure who had confronted him on the stairs. He felt something stirring inside him.

'She must be a most unusual governess, then!' laughed Percy.

'She is,' said James thoughtfully. He remembered the flash in Miss Davenport's eyes as she had told him she was not a house-maid but a governess. And he remembered something else: the unwelcome effect that flash had had on his body.

He shifted uncomfortably in his seat.

'Miss Davenport,' he said, under his breath, 'is a most unusual governess indeed.'

CHAPTER THREE

Sarah dressed with great care the following morning. She rejected her two old muslin dresses and chose instead her new sarsenet gown. She had bought the length of sea-green sarsenet in London, with money Lady Templeton had kindly given her as an advance on her first month's wages. It had lain at the bottom of her wardrobe for the first ten days, all but forgotten as Sarah had adjusted to her new life. But then she had taken it out and had occupied herself in the evenings by turning it into a simple gown.

She had always been skilled with a needle and had enjoyed sewing the new styles which, after a break of many years, had come from Paris once again. Now that Napoleon was safely imprisoned on Elba and King Louis was back on his throne, Paris had reclaimed its place in the *ton*'s affections, and although Sarah had never visited the city herself—and was never likely to!—she had been able to see the Parisian fashions on fashionable ladies in town. The skirt of her gown was slightly flared, clearing the ground instead of trailing on it; a practical feature that, in her present circumstances, she much appreciated. The neckline was round and, like the puffed sleeves, was decorated with a frill.

All in all, as she surveyed herself in the cheval-glass, she was pleased with the result. The sea-green brought out the unusual shade of her green eyes and complemented her auburn hair, which she had arranged neatly in a bun. And because the dress was new, it gave her confidence; confidence she would need if she was to stand up to Lord Randall: he was indeed an arrogant and highhanded man!

She picked up a sample of Lucy's work, being pleased that she had made the little girl work on paper as well as on slates so that she had something to show her employer. Then, with a final smooth of her hair, she left her room and went downstairs. The long-case clock in the hall began to strike eight o'clock.

It was already hot, the early summer sunshine pouring in through the mullioned windows and lighting up the heavy panelling, bringing the imposing hall and stairs to life.

On the sixth stroke Sarah reached the bottom of the stairs; on the seventh she reached the door of the study; and on the eighth she knocked on the door and heard Lord Randall's voice calling, 'Come in.'

'Ah! Miss Davenport,' he said, looking up briefly as she entered the room.

He was standing by his desk with a pile of papers in his hand. Further papers covered the desk.

'Please, sit down,' he said.

'Thank you,' she said. But she knew that she needed every inch of height if she was to stand up to him. 'I prefer to stand.'

He looked surprised; then curious; then nodded, saying, 'As you wish.'

He was looking immaculate. There was nothing dishevelled about his clothes as there had been the day before, at the end of his long and tiring journey. Instead they were fresh and crisp. His cream breeches were stretched tightly across his powerful legs and disappeared into highly polished Hessians. He wore no coat, because of the heat, but his fine linen shirt was stiff with starch.

It was complemented by a cravat, expertly arranged in an intricate set of folds—a waterfall.

There was no hint of bronzed skin showing beneath the neck of his shirt as there had been the day before, when he had pulled his cravat awry in order to loosen his top two buttons;

nothing to lessen the effect of a formidable earl, with black hair, black eyes and a strong sense of presence; an earl who was used to getting his own way.

'Now,' he said, turning his attention to Sarah, 'we'll discuss your duties. It's a pity I hadn't had a chance to read Lady Templeton's letter before I spoke to you yesterday, but as long as you're suitable for the position I've decided to let you stay. You speak French, I take it?' he asked, speaking as though this was the most basic of accomplishments.

'A little,' said Sarah. She was on her mettle and did not intend to give him any more help than necessary. If she let him get the upper hand he would certainly use it!

'Only a little?' he asked, raising one black eyebrow.

She nodded.

'And what do you think of the children?' he threw at her in French.

'I think they are willing, intelligent and well behaved,' she answered him, also in French; but her accent was not as good as his.

'As you say,' he remarked with a wry smile. 'You speak French "a little". And how about music?' he asked her. 'You play the piano, I take it? And the harp?'

'The harp, no. But I play the piano—a little.'

'Tell me, Miss Davenport,' he said, with a lift of his eyebrows, 'is there anything you do more than "a little"?'

'I care about the children more than a little,' she returned, annoyed at his high-handed attitude. He may not have appointed her, and he may have some grounds for criticizing her accomplishments, but he didn't have any right to treat her as though she was a scullery-maid. And an unsatisfactory scullery-maid at that!

'You're not employed to care about the children,' he returned without thinking, annoyed that she had answered him back.

'Yes I am. In fact, that's exactly why Lady Templeton appointed me. Because she recognized that the children need someone who cares for them. They need someone who realizes that they are children and not tin soldiers.' She braced herself as she saw him frown. He may not want to hear what she wanted to say, but for the good of the children she was determined to speak her mind. 'The boys are already being well taught by their tutors, and Lucy won't need an accomplished governess until she's older. But what she *does* need is someone who will allow her to be a little girl instead of expecting her to behave like a doll. And the boys need someone who will allow them to be children before it is too late.'

'You seem to have very decided views on the needs of children for one so young,' he remarked angrily, adding bitingly, 'You speak, of course, from experience.'

Sarah felt a flush spreading over her cheeks. She knew that his sardonic remark was intended to silence her, but in fact it had the opposite effect. There was something about this arrogant man that challenged her and she took up the gauntlet he had thrown down.

'As a matter of fact I do. I looked after my two younger brothers when my mother became an invalid and I know how important it is for children to play, as well as to work.'

'You have two brothers?' he asked in surprise. It had not occurred to him that she might have younger brothers. 'Who is taking care of them now?'

Sarah felt her spirits fall. The thought of her forced separation from her dearly loved brothers always made her low. She spoke quietly, the heat gone from her voice. 'When my father died, they were adopted by my aunt and uncle.'

'Whilst you were left to fend for yourself?' he asked curiously.

'Yes.'

He looked at her thoughtfully. 'I see.'

She sighed. It was an old wound, but it was still capable of giving her pain. 'No. I don't think you see at all.'

Her reply was so unexpected that, instead of being angry, he found that he was intrigued. He looked at her intently, as though he did not know what to make of her; it was possibly the first time in his life—other than to note an exceptional face or figure—that he had ever really looked at *any* woman; as though he wanted to know what went on inside her mind.

She was, he realized, a puzzle. She did not fit any pattern of womanhood that he knew. Usually he could fit any new female into a definite type: quaking governess, toad-eating social climber, deferential servant, complacent society hostess, hopeful débutante, flattered married woman, promiscuous widow. But Miss Davenport did not fit any of these types. She was a young lady with a completely original mind.

He shook his head.

Miss Davenport might be original, but a governess had no business being original. Her only business was to teach the children in her care.

'The children's timetable will be as follows,' he said abruptly, throwing his sheaf of papers down on to the desk and walking over to the window; reminding himself that Miss Davenport's life outside the classroom was none of his concern. 'The boys will be taught by their tutors until five o'clock every day.' He found that he could see her reflection in the window-pane and turned away. The sight of her was too distracting! Her face, whilst not conventionally beautiful—far less beautiful than Margaret's, in fact—was strangely attractive, with intelligent eyes and expressive features, whilst her body had the most delicate and subtle curves . . .

He marshalled his thoughts, and then continued. 'Once their tutors have left the Grange, the boys will be your responsibility for the rest of the evening, that is until you hand them over to the nurse so that she can put them to bed. I expect their activities to be educational—I'm determined that they will not miss out on their education just because they are being taught at home. You will teach Lucy the basic subjects in the morning, and will devote your afternoons to teaching her music, needlework and dancing. The children will take some exercise in both the morning and the afternoon. They will take a walk in the morning, and will march along the terrace in the afternoon. They should enjoy that,' he added thoughtfully, remembering how he had loved to pretend to be a soldier when he had been a boy.

'And when will the children play?' asked Sarah innocently.

'You seem to be obsessed with the idea of playing,' he said, turning round in exasperation. Why would this governess not simply do as she was told? 'And, no! Don't tell me about your brothers,' he said, seeing that she was about to do so. 'Their situation wasn't anything like the situation of the children at Watermead Grange.'

'They were the sons of a gentleman,' returned Sarah with a sudden flash in her eyes:

it was one thing for him to ridicule her accomplishments, but quite another for him to belittle her brothers.

That flash—a brilliant illumination of her eyes—had a profound effect on his body, making it difficult for him to concentrate on what she was saying.

'They worked hard,' he heard her go on, 'but that didn't mean they never had time to play.'

'They didn't stand to inherit the Watermead estate,' he reminded her.

'But you did,' countered Sarah, rising to the challenge once again. 'Did it mean you never had time to play?'

'That is not the point.'

'It's exactly the point.'

'Miss Davenport,' he said, finding himself, for the first time in his life, out of his depth; not knowing how to deal with the young woman before him, a young woman who was like no young woman he had ever encountered before. 'Are you always so argumentative?'

'Only when I'm arguing for something I believe in. Children are children.' She realized belatedly that she was doing everything she had told herself she would not do; responding emotionally to the darkly handsome man before her, when she had meant to speak to him in a calm and businesslike way. She took a deep breath and steadied her rapidly beating pulse. 'If the children are treated with too much discipline, they will rebel. Or, even worse, they won't have the strength to resist and they'll submit; and once they've done that, their spirits will be broken. And that is a terrible fate.'

Spirits? Submit? Rebel? What was she talking about?

Lessons and accomplishments; handwriting and deportment; these were the things governesses spoke to him about—when they dared speak to him at all! But here was Miss Davenport talking to him about spirit, and rebellion, and submission, of all things. He did not know what to make of it.

Or of her.

His eyes roamed over her face. It was an ordinary face—wasn't it? Giving no outward sign of her uniqueness. Unless it could be traced in her intelligent eyes, the surprisingly beautiful line of her cheek, the curve of her lips, or the provocative tilt of her chin . . .

But what was he thinking?

She was a governess.

He had no interest in the curve of her lips or the tilt of her chin—as he firmly reminded himself. His only interest lay in her ability to do her job.

And he would only discover how great that ability was by seeing what Lucy had learned.

The sight of the books brought his thoughts back to where they should be, and he wondered how he could ever have let the interview get so out of hand.

'You've brought me some of Lucilla's work, I see.'

Sarah let out her breath. She felt a store of pent-up tension rush out of her. Lord Randall had been looking at her so intensely that she had forgotten to breathe but now, to her relief, the disturbing look had left his eyes.

Even so, as she handed him the books, her instincts warned her not to let her hand touch his . . .

Lord Randall seated himself behind his desk and waved his free hand towards a shield-backed chair.

Sarah hesitated for a moment and then sat down. She didn't fully understand what had just happened to her, but nevertheless she discovered she was feeling weak and she was glad she no longer had to stand.

Lord Randall fell silent as he looked through Lucy's books.

To Sarah's surprise, he soon became absorbed. She had expected him to give the books a cursory glance and then make some scathing comment, but he did no such thing. He looked at the books—really looked—taking a genuine interest in everything he saw; and Sarah, as well as being glad of the interest he was taking for Lucy's sake, was glad of the opportunity it gave her to recover her composure. Because, she had to admit, she needed it. But as her thoughts began to settle, and as her breathing and heartbeat began to resume their usual regular pattern, she saw with relief that Lord Randall was truly interested in the little girl and she began to believe that there was hope for their future encounters. They would not all be so angry, she hoped!

Lord Randall continued to study the books. At last he looked up and said in surprise, 'These are good; these are very good. I'd never realized Lucilla could write so neatly—or invent such interesting stories.'

'Her writing's coming on by leaps and bounds.' Sarah smiled, glad to be able to tell Lord Randall how well Lucy was doing. 'Her singing's coming on, too. She's very musical and loves to learn new songs.'

He gave a reluctant smile. 'It seems there is something you can do more than "a little", Miss Davenport; it seems that you can *teach*.'

Sarah glowed with the unexpected praise. She loved her job, and no matter how chagrined she was to discover it, Lord Randall's appreciation warmed her. 'With such an interested little girl it's hard to go wrong.'

His expression softened. So much so that he looked almost human! 'She's a good child,' he said. 'They are all good children. It's such a tragedy that . . .'

He stopped himself, and for a few moments he became lost in thought.

Then, rousing himself, he said, 'Well, you

have made a good start, Miss Davenport. I'll be keeping an eye on the children's progress whilst I am at the Grange. But now I mustn't keep you. You have your duties to attend to'—he looked ruefully at the papers littering his desk—'as I have mine.'

Sarah recognized her dismissal.

'Very good, my lord,' she said, rising.

'Oh, Miss Davenport,' he called after her as she reached the door. 'There is just one other thing . . .'

'My lord?' She turned round.

Standing there he looked extremely handsome, with the sun painting blue highlights into his black hair. And his features . . . was it possible? Could he actually be—*smiling*?

It changed his face, making him seem younger; more relaxed; less arrogant. His smile broadened and his voice was warm. 'Welcome to Watermead Grange.'

*　　*　　*

The top floor of the Grange was used for a number of purposes. Part of it was used as servants' quarters; part of it was used for storage; but the rest was given over to the children's rooms. Here, too, were the schoolrooms: Fitzwilliam's and Preston's small studies and the larger room in which Sarah taught Lucy. The large room was clean and sound, and because of its size it was cool for most of the day; at least until the evening, when the sun moved round and shone into the west-facing window.

Sarah often remained in the schoolroom at four o'clock, whilst Lucy, watched over by her nurse, had a rest. There she would mark the day's work or prepare Lucy's lessons for the following day, before taking charge of all three children for the early part of the evening, when the boys' daily tutors left the Grange.

The only drawback to this arrangement was that Mr Haversage had discovered it, and was beginning to become a nuisance.

Mr Haversage was the boys' tutor, and was responsible for teaching them general subjects, as well as Latin and Greek. There were other tutors who came in for a few hours each day to give the boys lessons in mathematics and the sciences, but it was Mr Haversage who was mainly in charge.

At a quarter to five he walked into the room.

He was a good-looking young man in his early twenties and was, as always, immaculately dressed. The colours he wore were pale, and Sarah had the distinct impression they had been chosen to complement his fair colouring. His hair was a pale-straw colour; his eyes were blue and cool. Despite his brilliance—he was an Oxford man—he had nothing of the air of an academic about him. Instead he had the air of an ambitious young man for whom teaching was just the start.

He was not particularly well liked by the boys, though the housemaids adored him. But for all his undoubted good looks, Sarah, in common with the boys, did not like the man.

'Fitzwilliam and Preston will be along shortly,' he told her. It was the custom for him to send the boys to the schoolroom at five o'clock. 'They are just finishing off a piece of Latin prose.'

Sarah mumbled a vague reply. She was absorbed in what she was doing and wanted to finish before Lucy returned with her nurse.

'Your interview with Lord Randall went well, I hope?' asked Mr Haversage, going over to the globe which perched on Sarah's desk and giving it a spin.

'As well as can be expected. Although I find it difficult to imagine why he has such difficulty in understanding his own children,' she said thoughtfully as she marked Lucy's maths.

'His own . . .' Mr Haversage stopped abruptly, and gave a grin.

Sarah, however, was engrossed in what she was doing and did not see his expression.

'His own children,' repeated Mr Haversage.

So, the governess had assumed the children were Lord Randall's brats, had she? A natural enough assumption to make. And one the housekeeper and the rest of the staff would never correct, because the housekeeper, that self-righteous madam, wouldn't allow the servants to gossip about their master.

His grin widened. Here was an opportunity for making trouble, indeed.

'These great men,' he said, deliberately encouraging her mistake. 'They never care about anyone but themselves.' He gave the globe another spin.

'Do you mind?' Sarah sighed, putting her hand on the globe to stop its whirling. She was annoyed by his habit of interfering with her things, but knew better than to make an issue of it. Nonetheless, she wished he would go away.

Sensing her feelings, Mr Haversage settled himself on the desk.

'That looks interesting,' he said, looking over her shoulder at the work she was preparing.

He was very close to her, and Sarah could feel his breath on her neck. The sensation made her uneasy. There was something about him that she simply did not like, and in order to get him to move away from her she said sharply, 'You're in my light.'

'We can't have that, can we?' There was a mocking note in his voice. 'The conscientious governess must have her work finished on time.'

She looked round impatiently. 'Do you have anything to say to me, or are you just bored?'

she asked.

'I wouldn't need to be bored to talk to you.' He perched himself on the edge of her desk and thrust his hands into his pockets and said banteringly, 'My only concern is that you don't talk back.'

But Sarah had no intention of bantering with him. She felt unhappy at his closeness and could feel the small hairs on the back of her neck rising. 'I'm busy,' she said.

'You won't be busy next Friday.'

'I'm always busy on a Friday,' she remarked, making an exclamation of annoyance as a large blob of ink dropped from the end of her quill and blotted her page.

'Not next Friday. You've been here almost a month now. It will be your afternoon off.'

Sarah stopped in the middle of sanding her paper. She was surprised. But a moment's reflection told her that what he said was true.

'What will you do with the time?' he asked her.

'I hadn't really thought about it.'

'There are some interesting ruins just a few miles to the north of here. They're surrounded by trees; cool and shady. I'd be happy to show them to you if you like. I know them well.'

'No—thank you,' she added. She often seemed to add a belated thank you when speaking to Mr Haversage. His remarks somehow always made her uneasy and her first reaction was to shoot out a curt reply.

'Why not?'

Sarah had the disturbing feeling he was enjoying her discomfiture.

She shrugged. 'I have other plans.'

'And what are they?' he asked her, as though challenging her to produce any.

'They—are my own concern.'

'A pity.' He stood up suddenly as Lucy and her nurse entered the room. 'Perhaps another time.'

Sarah made no reply, but she was not sorry to see him leave. She was probably over-reacting, but still, she did not like Mr Haversage's company and was happy that Lucy had returned.

'Are we going to play in the woods?' asked Lucy, as her nurse followed Mr Haversage out of the room.

Sarah hesitated. Lord Randall might not see the value of play, but he had not expressly forbidden her to let the children indulge in normal childhood games. And besides, she had managed to establish a more friendly relationship with him towards the end of the morning's interview. If any difference of opinion arose between them in the future Sarah felt confident they would be able to sort it out. Her hesitation lasted only for a moment, after which she responded to Lucy's open arms with a hug and said, 'Yes. We'll have to wait for the boys, but as soon as they arrive we'll go outside.'

Preston was the next to arrive, followed closely by Fitzwilliam, and together the small party made its way down to the woods which lay behind the house. In the weeks that Sarah had been at Watermead Grange the boys had lost their reserve, and were now happy and confident in her company. Lucy, too, had flourished, and was quickly developing into a confident and capable little girl.

It was pleasantly cool in the woods. The large trees were fully leaved, and created a welcome sea of shade away from the glare of the sun. The children, who had been rather limp after a day spent indoors, began to revive. Before long they were running about, playing hide-and-seek, with Lucy, as the youngest, being given the first turn to hide.

It was a game that Sarah knew would occupy them for some time. She settled herself comfortably beneath one of the trees and, after watching the children play for a while, she turned her attention to a piece of embroidery she had brought with her. It was a cross-stitch picture, showing two birds fluttering through a wooded background; perfect for her present location.

She selected a length of blue cotton and threaded her needle, then began to stitch. The repetitive work was soothing, and she thought how lucky she had been to find such an enjoyable post. She loved teaching Lucy, and to be able to teach her in such pleasant surroundings was fortunate indeed.

She was just about to finish off and call the children, telling them it was time to return to the house, when she heard voices. One she recognized immediately as the voice of Lord Randall. The second, a man's voice, was one she did not know; but, as they drew nearer and she caught some of their conversation, she realized he must be the estate manager.

In another minute the two gentlemen were upon her. She stood up to greet them. After the friendly ending to her interview with Lord Randall Sarah felt she could meet him with confidence. But then she saw the expression on his face and her spirits sank.

'Shouldn't you be looking after the children?' he asked, as he found her in the woods apparently alone.

'Oh, I am,' she hastened to reassure him. She could not blame him for being angry if he thought she had abandoned her duty.

'I don't see them,' he said, glancing round the woods.

Thinking some humour would lighten the situation and prevent it from developing into another battle, Sarah said with a smile, 'You're not meant to. They are playing hide-and-seek!'

But Lord Randall, mistaking her humour for levity, thought she was taking advantage of the friendliness he had shown her at the end of that morning's interview—and what had he been doing, being friendly to a governess? he asked himself vexedly—and a frown crossed his face.

'If you'll excuse me, my lord,' said Dawson, the estate manager, who was beginning to feel distinctly out of place. 'I'd better see to the drainage.' He hurried away.

'You were told to make sure that the children's occupations were educational,' said Lord Randall as soon as Dawson was out of hearing. 'I thought I had made myself clear.'

'An hour spent in the woods is educational,' she said, trying not to fight him but at the same time needing to make him understand. 'Children aren't like adults. They can't spend all their time working. They need time to run about and be free. They need time to enjoy themselves. They need time to *play*.'

'We have had this conversation before,' he said, angry that she was deliberately flouting his wishes.

'And will no doubt have it again,' she flashed.

'I am not in the habit of having my decisions questioned,' he said warningly, looking suddenly larger and darker than ever before.

'Then perhaps it's a habit you should get into,' she returned, determined not to be intimidated.

But as soon as she had spoken she knew she had made a terrible mistake. It was one thing for her to tell Lord Randall that the children needed to be free to play; it was quite another for her to tell him that he should accustom himself to having all his decisions questioned; and questioned by a governess! She hadn't meant to say it, but he had antagonized her and the words had been out of her mouth before she could stop them.

At once his face closed, and she knew he would not listen to anything else she had to say. If she had handled the situation differently, if she had not let her tongue run away with her, then she could have reasoned with him. But she had antagonized him by her outspokenness and the opportunity for a calm discussion had slipped away.

'I honoured your appointment because you are a gifted teacher,' he said arrogantly, 'but if you wish to keep your position I suggest you rethink your attitude. The children's free time will be spent educationally in the future. That is my final word on the subject. If you do not feel you can cope with this requirement then I will be happy to accept your resignation. And now, Miss Davenport, I will bid you good day.'

He strode away.

Insufferable man! thought Sarah, as she watched his receding figure disappear amongst the trees.

And insufferable idiot, came her next thought miserably as she was forced to admit that she had made a fool of herself. She, the governess, thinking she could tell Lord Randall what to do!

She sighed. She was finding it very difficult to remember that she was no longer Miss Davenport, gentleman's daughter, but Miss Davenport, governess.

Somehow her previous position as a companion had not been as trying. Although once or twice she had spoken out of turn, in general she had been able to control herself. There had been nothing, after all, but her own feelings at stake. But here it was different. Here the children's happiness was at stake.

Even so, she did not know how she could have let her tongue run away with her like that. She was lucky she had not been dismissed.

A rebellious part of her thought that, for two pins, she would be happy to give in her notice. But even as she thought it she knew it wasn't true. She had become too attached to the children to want to leave them. And besides, if she left Watermead Grange, where else did she have to go?

* * *

'A penny for them, James,' said Maud de Bracy later that evening, as Lord Randall stood broodingly by the fireplace once dinner was over.

She and Percy were enjoying their stay at Watermead Grange and had spent a pleasant day idling about the house and grounds. But now Maud was in the mood for conversation with her handsome host, and she made an effort to engage his attention.

'Hm?'James asked, turning his coal-black eyes towards her.

Those eyes are what women pine for, she thought, as she looked into their depths. But he's completely unaware of their fascination.

'You've been distracted all evening,' she told him.

'Yes, James, it's true,' said Percy. He fumbled tunelessly on the piano. 'We've had hardly a word out of you all evening. Is anything wrong?'

'Nothing.' He crossed over to the small table at the side of the room where the drinks were laid out and helped himself to a brandy. After which he stood looking out of the window. Dusk had fallen, casting a soft grey light over the terrace and the lawns beyond. But he did not see the view. Instead, he saw a scene that had played itself out before his eyes earlier that evening, after his encounter with Miss Davenport. He had been striding angrily back towards the house, his anger directed as much at himself for losing his temper as it was directed at Miss Davenport for ignoring his wishes, when he had caught sight of Fitzwilliam, and the sight of Fitzwilliam as he had never seen him before had rooted him to the spot. Because Fitzwilliam had not been walking along listlessly as he usually did;

Fitzwilliam had been racing along at top speed. Having abandoned their game of hide-and-seek the children had moved on to a game of tag, and as James swirled the brandy in his glass he recalled how Fitzwilliam had raced through the woodland, laughing and breathless, before veering to the left and climbing up the trunk of a nearby tree, crying out in triumph, 'Home!' Fitzwilliam, who had always seemed so vacant; Fitzwilliam, who said, 'Yes, my lord,' and, 'No, my lord,' in the politest way possible, but who never really seemed to be really *there.* And that was the boy who had raced through the woodland with an expression of delight on his face; who had outstripped his more spirited brother; and who had been completely, utterly *alive.*

Could it be that he had been wrong about the children? Could his ideas have been misguided, no matter how well intentioned they had been?

He swirled the brandy round his glass. As he did so his thoughts drifted back to his confrontation with Miss Davenport earlier that morning. He remembered her telling him that the children must be given more freedom if their spirits were not to be crushed; that they must be allowed to play. He had not known what she meant at the time, but he knew now. It seemed she was an even better governess than he had supposed.

It must have taken courage for her to stand

up to him like that, he thought. And to defend her beliefs. He remembered the spark in her eye when she had openly defied him . . . the shape of her mouth, the arch of her neck . . .

He turned his thoughts away. He couldn't allow himself to be attracted to her. Those feelings would complicate things.

Complicate, but not change them. Because no matter how attractive he found her he did not intend to let a governess tell him what he could and could not do.

Except—

'James! James!' Maud's insistent voice broke in on his thoughts. 'Do come over here and stop Percy murdering the piano!'

With a sigh he turned away from the window, and reluctantly gave his attention to his guests.

CHAPTER FOUR

Sarah was in her small private sitting-room a few days later, preparing a nature lesson for Lucy. The sitting-room was connected to her bedroom by a door, and the two rooms formed the small suite she had been given on her arrival at the Grange. It was furnished in similar style to the bedroom, with oddly assorted furniture of good quality—it was Lord Randall's custom to have good pieces of furniture moved into the upper servants' quarters when he replaced them with something better. There was a padded armchair, a slipper-chair, a shield-backed chair and a *chaise-longue.* There was also a small desk. Sarah was sitting at the desk, and had been sitting there for almost half an hour, but she was still no nearer to thinking up a lesson for Lucy. She had wanted the little girl to make a collection of plants, but there were a number of specimens around the Grange that Sarah did not recognize herself. She would have to think of something else. Unless . . . unless there were any botany books in the library which might help her find out what she wanted to know.

She set down her quill, but at that moment a knock came at the door and a minute later Nelly, one of the housemaids, entered the room.

'There's a letter for you, miss,' said Nelly, bobbing a curtsy. 'It got mixed up with the master's letters. You should have had it this morning, miss. But better late than never, they do say.'

'Yes, Nelly. Thank you,' said Sarah, taking the precious letter. And then, as Nelly seemed inclined to linger, she said, 'Thank you, Nelly. That will be all.'

The girl bobbed a curtsy and left the room.

Sarah looked at the letter. She recognized the handwriting at once. It was from her younger brother, Nicholas. Abandoning her work she took the letter over to the window-seat and, settling herself comfortably against the cushions, she began to read.

The letter was full of news, and as Sarah read it she felt she was almost with Nicholas in her uncle's home in Bath. He had bought a new phaeton, she discovered—she suppressed a sisterly pang as she hoped he would not drive it too fast—and had taken Geoffrey, their younger brother, for a jaunt around Bath. Geoffrey was doing well at university, and had passed all his summer exams. Uncle Hugh was as drunk as ever, and Aunt Claire was gossiping her time away in the Assembly Rooms and Spring Gardens.

Imagine Geoffrey doing so well at university, thought Sarah, as she finally folded the letter and put it away in her desk with the others. He had never been interested in studying as a boy, but to her surprise he had taken to Cambridge like a duck to water. She gave a sigh as she thought how proud her parents would have been. They would have loved to have seen Nicholas as a man about town, and would have been delighted with Geoffrey's achievements.

But there was no use repining. She reminded herself that she had work still to do, and went down to the library in search of books on botany.

* * *

'The barn's been mended, m'lord, as you wanted,' said Ben Higgins, the estate carpenter, 'but the bridge is going to be a bigger job. The wood's all rotten, beggin' your pardon, m'lord, and the timber'll need replacing if it's to be made all right and tight again.'

'Very well,' said Lord Randall. He was looking out towards the small lake that was spanned at its narrow end by the ornamental bridge. 'But I want it doing before the end of the month. It must be finished before my guests arrive.'

'Yes, m'lord.'

'Oh, and tell Jenkins I want to see him first thing in the morning,' went on Lord Randall, referring to the stonemason. 'There are a number of things that need his attention. And tell him to bring his tools.'

'Yes, m'lord. Very good, m'lord.'

'All right, Higgins. You can go now; that will be all.'

'Very good, m'lord,' said Ben.

Lord Randall finished sorting out a pile of papers which were arranged with military precision on the top of his desk, then gave a last glance around the room. Everything that had needed doing had been done—at least for today. The rest could wait until the morning.

Then, as was his custom when he had no

visitors—Maud and Percy had left for Sussex—he went to the library, where he intended to while away the remainder of the evening.

The sun, less intense than it had been over the last few days, was by this time low in the sky. It slanted in through the mullioned windows, casting a rosy glow over the break-fronted bookcases and the spines of the well-worn leather books. It caught the gold lettering which spelt out the names of the authors and the titles of the books, making it gleam. And it also caught something else. It caught the strands of Miss Davenport's auburn hair.

Lord Randall checked on seeing her. The feelings he had experienced only a few short days before, feelings no man as proud as he was should ever experience for a governess—especially a man who was as good as betrothed—made him unwilling to find himself alone with her. But at the same time he knew it was the perfect opportunity for him to tell her that he had decided the children should, after all, be allowed to play. He had given the matter a lot of thought and having seen how confident Fitzwilliam had become, and how much happier Lucy and Preston seemed, he had realized that he was wrong and she was right. And difficult though it was, he knew he must admit it.

Looking at her as she stood examining the

books in the westering sunlight, he found that, unaccountably, he was looking forward to their meeting.

At that moment she looked up and saw him.

'Lord Randall!'

She clutched at the book which, in her first moment of surprise, she had almost let fall. She was not normally a clumsy person, but she felt a sudden change in the atmosphere and temporarily lost control of herself.

He took a step towards her, catching the book. She took it quickly; but not quickly enough to prevent his hand from brushing hers. A tingling sensation passed up her arm and down her spine. She felt suddenly awkward, and she wanted to explain her presence in the library. 'I came in to get some books on botany,' she said. 'I didn't realize you would be wanting the library this evening.'

She waited apprehensively for his reply. She felt on edge with him; breathless; not knowing what direction their meeting would take. She remembered their last encounter clearly, and although she knew that she had been right about the children and he had been wrong, she knew she shouldn't have spoken to him as she had done. She also knew that, despite his anger, he had been very lenient with her: many other employers would have dismissed her on the spot.

With these feelings uppermost in her mind she felt that it was unfortunate he had just walked into the library. She had been hoping to avoid him, as Lady Templeton had all but advised her to do, so that there would be no more arguments. And if there were no more arguments then, as soon as the house-party was over and he had left the Grange, she would once again be able to let the children play.

And she would be able to recover her composure, which seemed to be rattled whenever Lord Randall was near.

Gathering up the books she had chosen she made to walk past him, but he did not move out of her way.

'Those look interesting,' he said, looking at the books she was carrying. 'I didn't know you were fond of botany.'

Was she mistaken, Sarah wondered, or was there a hint of a smile around his full lips?

Unable to stop it, her mouth broke into a smile all of its own. 'I'm not.' She tried unsuccessfully to suppress a gurgle of laughter.

To her surprise—and intense relief—her laughter did not incense him. In fact, his own smile broadened.

'Then why the books?' he asked.

'I'm preparing one of Lucy's lessons.'

'At this late hour?' He was surprised.

'It's cooler to work in the evenings,' she explained. 'Besides, it isn't as if I have anything better to do.'

'Oh, yes, you have,' he said, surprising

himself almost as much as he surprised her. 'You can stay a while and talk to me. If, that is,' he said, again with a smile, 'you think that is better than preparing one of Lucy's lessons!'

Sarah smiled, and the curve of her mouth drew his eye. It really was most deliciously shaped . . . He took the heavy books from her and put them in a pile on top of the finely-carved lectern. He motioned her towards one of the Hepplewhite chairs drawn up beside a large writing-table, and when she had seated herself he sat opposite her, his firm legs stretched out in front of him.

The situation was proving easier than he had expected. When she was not bristling with anger—and when he was not angry either—they seemed to share a rapport, and this rapport would make it much easier for him to talk to her in the future.

Sarah, too, found the situation to be easier than she had expected. She did not know what to make of Lord Randall's change of manner, but she felt that now, whilst his softer mood lasted, it would be a good idea for her to make amends for her earlier angry outburst. 'I have something to say to you,' she began hesitantly. 'I—'

'No,' he said, interrupting her. 'Not before I have said something to you.'

He paused, seeming not to know how to continue.

When he had seen Sarah in the library he

had not known exactly what he would say. What he *had* known was that he must, somehow, let her know that she had been right about the children. But he was a proud man, and admitting that he had been wrong was not something that came easily to him. However, as well as being proud he was also fair, and no matter how difficult it was for him he knew it must be said.

'There's really no need . . .' began Sarah, when he didn't speak.

'Yes, there is. There's every need. You see . . .' He broke off and stood up, striding over to the mantelpiece. 'I'm not often wrong,' he said at last, 'but I was wrong the other day—'

'No,' said Sarah firmly. 'I was the one who was in the wrong. I should never have spoken to you like that.'

'No, you shouldn't,' he agreed. 'It was very wrong of you. In fact,' he added with a wicked smile, 'it was very impertinent!'

Sarah smiled, realizing that he was teasing her.

'But I was wrong, too,' he went on. 'You see, I caught sight of Fitzwilliam racing through the woods on my way back to the house. I've never seen him like that before. He's always been so . . .'

'Distant?' asked Sarah.

'Yes. Distant. But there was nothing distant about him then. He looked—alive.'

Sarah nodded. 'I know.'

'And it was you who brought him to life. I don't want the children behaving like ragamuffins, but a little play is'—he smiled—'a little play is perhaps something they need.'

'It is,' said Sarah. 'You must have needed to play yourself. I can't believe that learning to run the Grange meant you *never* had time to play.'

'You're right.' He returned to his chair. 'I used to play in the stables as a boy. I'd forgotten all about it until you reminded me.'

'You must have learnt a lot from the experience, as well as simply enjoying yourself,' said Sarah.

'How so?'

'Well, you must have learned how the horses were cared for, and how many jobs there were to be done, for example. And you must have learned a lot about the stable hands as well—which men worked well on their own, for instance, and which ones needed to be pushed. Then, too, you must have developed a respect for them, seeing how hard they worked. All important knowledge for a boy who was going to inherit an estate.'

He gave her a looked of mixed respect and surprise. 'Miss Davenport. Has anyone ever told you that you are a most *unusual* governess?'

Sarah gave a rueful smile. 'I never thought I'd be a governess at all. I thought . . .'

'Yes?' he asked, leaning forward in his chair.

He had known there was something unusual about her, that she was not a run-of-the-mill governess. Her father had been a gentleman, she had told him in an earlier encounter. Why had she been reduced to earning her own living?

'It doesn't matter what I thought.' She had become quieter. There was something almost wistful about her.

He sensed the change in her mood and did not press her further. Instead, he changed the subject and asked her, 'What made you apply for a job as a governess here? Did your family come from Kent?'

'Oh, no,' she told him, startled that he had made that assumption, although of course it was a perfectly natural one. 'In fact, I didn't apply for a job as a governess at all. I applied for a job as Lady Templeton's companion.'

Now it was his turn to look surprised.

'I had already worked as a companion, you see. When my father died my aunt and uncle adopted my brothers as they had no children of their own. They needed an heir—an heir and a spare, as my uncle put it—but they had no use for a girl. And so one of our neighbours in Derbyshire asked me if I would like to take care of her aunt. The old lady lived in London and needed someone to look after her, and so I travelled south. I stayed with her for a year, but sadly she died, and when she did so it seemed natural for me to seek another position as a companion. And so I applied for the position with Lady Templeton.'

There was an unusual look of compassion in James's eyes. 'It must have been hard for you,' he said, realizing how difficult Sarah's life had been and impressed by the lack of self-pity in her tone.

'Perhaps.' Sarah dismissed her problems lightly, although they had occasioned her much hardship. 'And then I went to see Lady Templeton. She told me I was too young to be her companion but I had already met Lucy by then, in one of the corridors. We had taken to each other and Lady Templeton offered me a post as her governess.'

'And do you like being a governess?' he asked.

'Yes, I do. Now that I know I don't have to speak Russian and play the harp, I like it very much indeed!'

He laughed, and she breathed a sigh of relief, because her tongue had run away with her again and she had not known how he would react to her teasing.

'You must find Kent very different from Derbyshire,' he said, on a different note. 'It's a tame and cultivated county, instead of being wild and remote. Not for nothing is it called the garden of England. Do you miss your home?'

'No.' She shook her head. 'I enjoyed growing up in Derbyshire. I loved playing on the high peaks when I was a little girl. But no, I don't miss it. The people I care about are no longer there. It's not my home any longer.'

He was interested to hear about her childhood. He had wondered how she had ever managed to develop such a determined personality and now he knew. If Miss Davenport had spent her childhood playing on the wild Derbyshire moors with her brothers, instead of sitting demurely at home with her mother, it was no wonder she had developed such a strong character and such an outspoken attitude to life. And if she had had to care for her brothers as her mother was an invalid, it was no wonder she knew so much about children—far more, in fact, than he did.

'I've travelled through the Peak District a number of times,' he said. 'It's very different from here, but I've always thought it beautiful.'

'It is. But in my mind it's too tied up with my mother's illness and my parents' death.' She stopped, wondering why she had confided such intimate thoughts to him. She continued in a more formal way. 'I can truly say I prefer Kent.'

His eyes lingered on hers. For such a young woman she had seen a lot of tragedy. He followed her eyes, which had turned towards the window, and the peaceful parkland that lay outside. He said, 'I love the Grange, and I hope Fitzwilliam will love it too.'

'He already does. He has told me he never

wants to leave.'

'Just wait until he is eighteen,' said Lord Randall. 'He will be pestering me to take him up to town and make him a member of White's. To say nothing of expecting me to introduce him to Gentleman Jackson at the gym! But afterwards, I hope he'll want to come back here.'

Sarah's thoughts, now that they had returned to the children, moved on to the work she still had to do. She had not prepared Lucy's lessons for the morning, and remembering that she still had a lot to do she stood up. 'I've already taken up enough of your time,' she said. 'If I want to have my lessons ready for tomorrow, I really must be getting on.'

Lord Randall made no objection—he had probably, thought Sarah, already spent more time on her than he had intended—and gave a brief nod. But as she made to pick up the pile of botany books he said, 'Have you read this?' He strode over to one of the bookcases and took a book of poetry from the shelves.

'*Childe Harold's Pilgrimage*,' she said, seeing what it was he had taken down. 'No, I haven't. I know everyone was talking about it at the time.' She remembered the stir Byron's work had caused when it had first appeared in 1812. 'But . . .'

She didn't finish her sentence. *But we had no money* to *spare for books*, she had been about to say, but she didn't want his pity and so she changed her mind.

'Take it with you,' he said, not noticing the tailing away of her sentence. 'I think you'll enjoy it.'

'Poetry?' asked Sarah, surprised.

'Don't you like poetry?' he asked.

'Yes, but . . .'

'But you thought I wouldn't. I do have *some* civilized habits,' he said with a wry smile.

Sarah smiled back. She had built her employer up into some sort of monster in her imagination, but she was beginning to realize that he was nothing of the kind. He did not take kindly to being crossed—and to be honest, who did?—but he was not as unreasonable as she had at first supposed.

She added the book to her pile. She would enjoy reading it, perhaps outside, in the evenings, once the children were in bed—at least, if the weather lasted.

She walked out of the library. As she did so she wondered how it was that a man she had dismissed as rude, arrogant and overbearing could turn out to have so many hidden depths to his character. And how it was that those depths stirred her in a way she had never been stirred before. Because being close to him had awakened in her new sensations and feelings; sensations she had not even known existed before her arrival at Watermead Grange.

CHAPTER FIVE

James glanced round the study. He had left everything in good order the previous evening but there was still a lot to be done.

He gave a sigh. The last thing he wanted was to be inside. The day was hot, and making matters even more difficult was the fact that Sarah was in the garden, playing with the children. A few days ago the sight would have angered him, but now he found that he would like nothing better than to go out and join them. So charming was the scene that, no matter how hard he tried to keep his mind on his work, his eyes kept drifting back to it.

Sarah was looking delightful in a spotted muslin that must have been at least three years old. How she contrived to look so delectable in such a shabby dress he did not know. It must be the subtle curves of her slim figure and the smoothness of her golden skin, he thought, that made him forget all about the worn nature of her clothes.

The children, too, were looking bright and happy as they laughed and played. Yes, it was a charming scene.

He gave a sigh and sat down at his desk: looking out of the window was not getting his work done. He had just finished checking the bills for repairs to the barn when the door opened and Hodgess entered the room.

'Mr Transom, my lord,' he announced.

'Dom?' James stood up, clasping his childhood friend by the hand as Dominic entered the room. It seemed he was fated to neglect his work that morning. Well, it would have to wait. 'Dom,' he said, clapping his friend on the back. 'It's good to see you again.'

Although the same age, the two men could not have been more different. Whilst James was dark, Dominic was fair, his hair bleached by the strong summer sun. His family owned one of the neighbouring estates, and the two men had played together as boys, spending their school holidays fishing or swimming or messing about in boats. But despite the fact that they were the same age, James had always had the stronger character, and had often saved his friend from childhood scrapes. It was James who had cautioned Dom against buying a 'first class horse' from 'an honest man in trouble' when they had been at Eton together, insisting that they should see the animal first; a good thing as it turned out, because the 'first class horse' had been in reality a knock-kneed, broken-winded toothless old nag. He had protected Dom from the card-sharps at university, and had saved him any number of untimely marriages, when Dom had taken pity on a serving-wench or been dazzled by a particularly voluptuous ladybird. So that, between them, they had had an enjoyable childhood and even more enjoyable university years.

Since then, their paths had crossed less often. Whilst James had been in the army, Dom had devoted himself to running his estate. But every time James had been home on leave the two men had met and renewed their friendship.

'I heard you were back,' said Dominic as Hodgess backed out of the room. 'I thought I'd ride over and pay a call.'

'I'm glad you did. I was coming over to see you myself this afternoon. Come in. Sit down—if you can find room,' said James glancing at the papers which seemed to cover every spare inch of space.

Dominic moved a sheaf of papers and sat down on a shield-backed chair. 'One of the perils of going away,' he said with a smile, looking at James's full desk.

'One of the many,' agreed James. 'But tell me, what's been happening whilst I've been away?'

The two men talked of general matters until at last James said, 'I'm glad you came over, Dom. Not just because I'm pleased to see you, but because I think you may be able to give me some information I need.'

Dominic gave him a curious look. 'Information?' There had been a more serious note to James's voice, and Dominic wondered what it meant. Surely James had left the army?

Surely now he was only interested in running the estate?

James threw down the quill with which he'd been toying and said, 'Yes. Information.' His mood had grown dark. 'Tell me,' he said, 'what do you know about the Radical Movement?'

Dominic's mood darkened, too. 'Not a lot. Only what everyone else knows. That the Radicals are unhappy with the government, and that they blame the politicians for unemployment and high taxes. They think their MPs are getting fat whilst they starve. And they're unhappy with royalty, too. They hate Prinny for his extravagance, and are angry that the money for his extravagances—the Pavilion down in Brighton, to name just one—comes out of the pockets of the poor.'

'Go on.'

'Well, they're not content to try and change things peacefully. They want to change things by force instead. When we had the war to bind us all together it was different, but now the war is over there's a lot of unrest.'

'If the Radicals manage to tap into the mood of unrest that's disturbing the country then they'll be capable of doing a great deal of harm,' said James, nodding. 'Some of them are reasonable, but a lot of them want to overthrow the old order and set up a new one in its place.'

'You think there's danger of a revolt?' asked Dom uneasily.

'Not at the moment, no. At the moment, the army is in England and it can stop any trouble before it gets out of hand. But if the army was to go back to the Continent . . .'

'But why would it do that?' asked Dominic with a frown. 'We've beaten Napoleon. He's imprisoned on Elba. The war's over, and we won.'

James was sombre. 'Against a man like Napoleon, I'm not sure it's ever possible really to win. As he said himself, he's one of those men who triumphs or dies.'

'You think . . .' Dom looked worried. 'You think Napoleon might escape? And start the war all over again?'

'I think it's possible, yes.'

'And if he does, the army will go back to the Continent and the Radicals will have free rein at home?' asked Dominic anxiously.

'It's not a certainty,' said James, seeing his friend's worried face. 'But the Radicals won't be sorry if Napoleon escapes. It will suit their purpose very well. In fact, we have reason to believe there are Radical agitators in Kent, conspiring with Napoleon's supporters to bring about that end.'

'I suppose it would be easy for them to keep in touch from here,' Dom admitted. 'There are so many coves that a small boat could easily put out undetected. The Radicals could keep in constant contact with Napoleon's friends.'

'Timing their own revolt to coincide with

Napoleon's escape. It's no more than a theory, a possibility, but with so much unrest in the country we have to take such possibilities into account.'

'We? You mean you, don't you? You and the army. You haven't really left.'

'I've sold my commission, but when help is needed, I offer it. I'm on the spot, Dom. I can't refuse. And that's where you come in. I need to know if there have been any new people in the neighbourhood recently. Anyone who might be a Radical.'

'No,' said Dominic definitely.

James gave a grim smile. 'Anyone at all? And don't forget, they wouldn't be likely to advertise the fact.'

'No, I suppose not.' Dominic thought for a moment. 'There *are* a few new people in the neighbourhood. There's the Reverend Mr Walker, but somehow I can't see him being mixed up in anything underhand.'

'A clergyman,' said James, nodding thoughtfully. 'It would be a good cover. Anyone else?'

Dominic pursed his lips. 'There are the Wilberforces. They're renting the Farbeys' estate. Farbey took some big losses at the gambling tables and was forced to let the house and fifty acres because of his debts. But I can't see them being involved. Mr Wilberforce collects butterflies, and his sister is involved in charitable works. Then there's

Charles Masterson. He's not strictly new but, like you, he's been in the army and has only just returned.'

'If his sympathies are with those who want change, then he could be a possible candidate,' said James. 'Is that all?'

'That's about it,' said Dominic. 'Except . . .'

'Except?' prompted James.

'Well, there is just one other person who's new to the neighbourhood.'

'And that is?'

Dominic hesitated. But James had asked for the names of anyone new to the neighbourhood. His eyes drifted to the window. 'Well . . . your governess.'

'Miss Davenport?' James looked out of the window. No, it was impossible. Or was it? Because Dominic was right: Miss Davenport was new to the neighbourhood. By rights he ought to treat her with the same suspicion as everyone else.

'Of course, I know you'd never hire a Radical. But you said you wanted to know about anyone who was new to the area, and Miss Davenport has only recently arrived.'

James pulled his eyes away from Sarah with difficulty. They had gone to her once more, but the scene no longer seemed so bright: a cloud had gone over the sun.

He turned his attention back to his friend. 'I think I'll hold a dinner party, Dom. To welcome my new neighbours to the area. Or better yet, an afternoon's boating. It will give me a chance to talk to them and sound out their beliefs. They won't give themselves away easily, but it's a rare man—or woman—who can talk for any length of time without making a single slip.'

'Can't it wait for the house-party?' asked Dominic.

'No. I'd rather have a look at my new neighbours first, without the distraction of a house full of guests. By the time the house-party comes round, I hope to have discovered who the Radicals are.'

* * *

Sarah was enjoying her game with the children. She had had very little exercise as a companion, but she was making up for it now! The boys were lively and energetic, and even Lucy kept her on her toes. Having spent the last ten minutes playing chase she was laughing and breathless, and was thankful when the stable clock struck twelve.

She gathered up her belongings—her battered bonnet and her needlework—and called the children over to her. 'Time to go in, children.'

'Aw!' said Preston, kicking the grass. 'Can't we stay out just a little bit longer?'

'Please,' said Fitzwilliam wheedlingly, whilst Lucy hopped up and down hopefully.

But Sarah was firm. 'No. Lunch will be almost ready. Come on, in we go.'

'Are you going into the village this afternoon?' asked Lucy, skipping along by Sarah's side as they went back to the house.

'I haven't decided yet but yes, I think I might.' It was Sarah's afternoon off, and she had the luxury of deciding what to do with the time. Much as she loved the children, it would be nice to do something for herself.

'If you do, you must remember to say hello to my duck. He's always on the duck-pond in the middle of the green. He's only got one leg, so he needs cheering up.'

Sarah smiled. Lucy's active imagination had already conjured up several interesting stories about George the one-legged duck, and Sarah promised to speak to this interesting personage if she did indeed go into the village.

As she neared the house she saw Lord Randall coming towards them. He was looking at her perplexedly, as though he was trying to find the answer to some question that was troubling him written on her face. But it probably had nothing to do with her, she told herself a minute later. It was probably just some problem with the estate.

'Miss Davenport,' he said as he joined them. 'I'd like a word with you, if I may?'

'Of course,' said Sarah. 'Run along, children, nurse will be waiting for you. And don't forget to wash your hands.'

The children took their leave and went into the house, where Lucy's nurse would supervise their lunch.

'Shall we?' asked Lord Randall, indicating the path that led to a charming gazebo. 'I won't keep you long,' he said as they strolled along, the heady perfume of the beautiful blooms beside the path filling the air. 'I know your time off must be precious. The children are enjoyable company, but they're also hard work. Have you decided what to do with your afternoon yet?'

'I thought I might walk down to the village. I've kept meaning to visit it but somehow I haven't got around to it yet. There are a number of purchases I'd like to make, and I've promised to say hello to Lucy's one-legged duck.'

He looked at her enquiringly.

'Lucy has adopted a one-legged duck. Apparently, he can be found on the duck-pond and, because of his infirmity, he needs cheering up.'

He laughed. 'Lucy is quite a character,' he said. 'You've really brought out the best in her. Do you know how to get to the village?' he asked.

'I think so. I was asking Mrs Smith for directions this morning. I turn left when I get out of the gates, don't I? And then just follow the road?'

'You can do. But after you've turned left

and followed the road a short distance you have a choice of ways. If you keep to the road then it's just straight on until you get there. But you can climb over a stile just before you reach the milestone and go the rest of the way on a narrow footpath through the fields if you prefer. It's shaded by hedgerows and will keep you out of the sun. And it will cut a mile off the walk.'

'I might try that, particularly on the way back.'

'But that was not what I wanted to talk to you about,' he said as they went into the gazebo. It was a charming octagonal building commanding a view down to the Watermead lake. A wooden seat ran round the interior of the building, and the walls were open above it, to provide glassless windows; a delightful feature on a summer's day.

'Miss Davenport,' he said, sitting opposite her, 'there is a matter on which I would like your advice.'

She put down her battered bonnet and gave him her attention.

He was looking more handsome than ever. Despite the apparent carelessness of his dress his presence was so strong that no one would have doubted who he was for a moment. He was very definitely the lord and master of the estate. And he was devastatingly handsome. Sarah tried to keep her mind on what he was saying, but his shirt was awry, revealing his tanned neck and an inch of tanned chest, and she found it distracting. She fixed her eyes on his face, focusing on the proud features: the high cheekbones, the black eyes and strong, full mouth; but her eyes wanted to wander downwards and trace the lines of his broad chest.

Why did she feel this way? she wondered. She had never had such disturbing thoughts about a man before.

'Miss Davenport,' he said, 'I am planning to host a boating afternoon so that I can meet my new neighbours and welcome them to Kent.' He watched her as he spoke, to see if there was any flicker of suspicion in her eyes. They remained wide and innocent, however, and he saw nothing to make him alarmed. 'There is a Mr Wilberforce and his sister, who are renting the old Farbey estate'—she showed nothing more than a polite interest in the names, he noted—'and the Reverend Mr Walker. Also a Mr Masterson.'

Again, there was nothing more than polite interest on her face.

As he did not continue, Sarah said, 'That sounds like a good idea, but I don't see why you need my advice.'

He leant forward, resting his elbows on his knees. 'I need to know whether you think Fitzwilliam is old enough to join us for the boating afternoon. He has spent the last year in the schoolroom, and I think a change would do him good.'

He had already formed the thought that Fitzwilliam was perhaps old enough to be introduced gradually into adult society—although he would have been the first to admit that, without Sarah's influence, the idea would not have occurred to him for some time—and it served as a convenient excuse for talking to Sarah and gauging her reaction to the names of people who might or might not be Radicals; and who might or might not be associates of hers. But he found that he was also genuinely interested to know what she had to say on the matter.

'I think he is,' she said at last. 'He can't spend his life with servants and tutors. He needs to know how to behave in polite society and yes, I think a small private boating party on his own estate would be a good occasion for him to learn.'

'Good. Then he will attend.'

'What about Preston?' she asked.

James shook his head. 'Preston is too young.'

'I don't think he is. He's only a year younger than Fitzwilliam, and this would be a good opportunity for him to see how adults behave in company. In fact Preston, being the more high-spirited of the two boys, probably needs the civilizing influence of society more than his brother.'

'You think that society has a civilizing

influence?' he asked, his attention caught.

'At its best, yes.'

'And at its worst?' he asked, his eyes narrowing. If she was a Radical then she would have a great deal to say about society at its worst, particularly about greedy MPs and princes who grew fat on the taxes of the poor.

'At its worst it encourages all manner of evils. Drunkenness, gambling, and worse.'

Drunkenness, gambling, and worse. These were not the evils the Radicals cared about. But still, he had to be sure.

'There are a lot of problems to be faced in life,' he said cautiously. 'Do you ever think we would do better to sweep the whole thing away and start again?'

'Like the French?' she asked.

He nodded, watching her closely.

She shook her head. 'No. There *are* a lot of problems to be faced in life, but I don't think a revolution can sweep them all away.'

'You don't think it's worth a try?'

'Like the Radicals, you mean?'

She asked the question openly, and he gave thanks for her outspoken nature. Sarah was not one to hide things away, to be devious and deceitful. She was straightforward and honest, and always spoke her mind.

'Yes.' He smiled; and was surprised to find that it was such a relief to have acquitted her of any connection with the Radicals.

'No. I don't think so. The French tried, and

only made matters worse. Besides, vices like drinking and gambling will always raise their heads. We can't protect the boys from them by sweeping them away. Instead, we have to teach them that gambling and drunkenness lead to a bad end, and hope that they are sensible enough to understand. Nothing in life is ever simple, after all, no matter who is in power.'

No. Nothing in life is ever simple, he thought. Least of all his feelings for her. Sarah should have been nothing but his niece's governess, and yet the relationship that was growing between them was coming to mean far more than he had ever dreamed possible. It was playing havoc with his emotions, and doing worse things to his body. Just to look at her was tempting. Her skin was so smooth and golden, her neck so beautifully sculpted and her breasts so tantalizingly curved that he could hardly restrain himself from touching her.

'We are agreed, then,' he said, realizing it would be safer to bring their conversation to an end. 'Fitzwilliam will join us for the boating afternoon. Can you make sure he knows what is expected of him?'

Sarah picked up her battered bonnet. 'I'll make sure both boys are fully prepared,' she said as she stood up.

'You have an uncanny knack of getting your own way where the children are concerned. I don't remember saying that Preston could join us.'

He had risen, too, and she had to look up to him.

'I have an uncanny knack of getting my own way when I am right,' she smiled.

His black eyes lit with a gleam of humour. 'I'm surprised that you don't make a plea for Lucy to join us.'

Sarah swung her bonnet by the ribbons, thinking. 'That might not be a bad idea. An afternoon in a boat will be enjoyable for her. And it will do her good to spend some time with you.'

Although it was not her place openly to criticize Lord Randall for spending so little time with the children, she felt she ought to do all in her power to encourage him to do so.

'Very well,' he agreed. 'As you will be there to keep an eye on her, I see no reason why she shouldn't join us.'

'I?' Sarah was startled.

'You don't think I'm going to keep an eye on the children myself? You are their governess. Of course you will be there.'

'But surely the boys' tutors . . .? Mr Haversage, perhaps—'

'Mr Haversage's presence will not be required. Yours, however, will.' He smiled as he saw her expression change. 'You look as though I have just suggested you should wrestle a bull!' Despite the fact that she was outspoken and never remembered her place, despite the fact that she told him what he could and could not do, despite the fact that she constantly challenged him, he found that, however much he wanted to, he could not be distant with her. And he could not stop his thoughts from wandering down wholly inappropriate channels, and wondering what it would be like to take her in his arms and taste the sweetness of her lips.

He tried to think of Miss Leatherhead as an antidote to these feelings, but somehow he found it difficult to call her to mind.

'I'm not sure that what you're asking me to do isn't worse,' she said; fortunately, for her own peace of mind, unaware of his thoughts. 'It's a long time since I've been in company, and my temper . . .'

She trailed off.

'Yes?' he enquired innocently. A humorous quirk lurked at the corner of his mouth.

'Sometimes I have trouble curbing my tongue!'

He laughed. 'I know! But you'll join us all the same, Miss Davenport.' Was there a hint of irony in his next comment, the slightest hint that he was laughing at himself? Or had she imagined it? she later wondered. Because his final words were: 'That is my command!'

* * *

Sarah's trip to the village had not been put off

by her conversation with Lord Randall, it had simply been delayed. After returning to the house for lunch and then collecting her gloves and reticule she set out for the village. The walk was very pleasant, the road being cool as it ran under overhanging trees for much of the way. She decided not to take the short cut, reserving it for the return journey so that she would have some variety in her walk.

At last the road led into the village. It consisted of a few shops, a vicarage, a blacksmith's and a church. The buildings were arranged round a small pond and a village green, and there in the middle of the pond was Lucy's duck. After saying hello to George, Sarah made her way to the milliner's. Now that she was to join the boating party she realized just how shabby her bonnet was, and she was looking forward to spending her wages on a new one. When worn with her new sarsenet dress, a new head-dress should make sure she was at least respectable at the gaiety.

'I'd like a new bonnet,' she said to the homely woman behind the counter, taking off her old one as she spoke.

Mrs Bridges recognized Sarah as a lady at once. She made her excuses and hurried into the back of the shop to fetch Miss Chester.

'Can I help you?' asked Miss Chester, emerging from the back room.

'I hope so!' said Sarah. 'I need a new bonnet . . .'

'Say no more,' said Miss Chester. She was delighted to have a lady to attend to; for, governess or no governess, it was clear that Sarah was a lady by birth. 'I have the very thing.'

In fact, she had a dozen or more 'very things', and Sarah spent an enjoyable half-hour trying on the latest bonnets. She dismissed a poke bonnet decorated with feathers and artificial flowers as being too impractical, and an Oldenberg bonnet—'as recommended in the *Ladies' Monthly Museum*', Miss Chester told her—as being too large. But a straw hat caught her eye. It was attractive yet practical, and would do a good job of keeping the sun off her face. It also had the advantage of being trimmed with a wide green ribbon which would complement the green of her new sarsenet gown, and she was feminine enough to be pleased with the fact that it matched the sea-green of her eyes.

'The very thing,' said Miss Chester as she made her choice. 'Straw hats are very fashionable at the moment, and if you should choose to change the ribbon at any time we have a large selection in stock.'

Sarah hesitated. Although her resources were small, the idea of the ribbon was tempting. She would then be able to match the hat to each gown she wore.

She succumbed to the temptation. Miss Chester fetched the box of ribbons; Sarah chose a primrose-yellow to go with her muslin and a turquoise to go with her spotted gown.

Though why I am taking all this trouble I really don't know, when I am nothing but a humble governess, she thought, ignoring the idea that it could have anything to do with Lord Randall. He was, after all, nothing but her employer, and it was unlikely he would even notice what colour ribbon she wore in her hat.

'Thank you for your custom,' said Miss Chester, handing Sarah her purchases. 'I hope to see you again.'

Standing outside the shop a few minutes later, Sarah toyed with the idea of walking home by the road. But she was tired, and decided to take the short cut. Carrying her hat-box in one hand and the rest of her other small purchases in the other, she soon found the point where the footpath began. Once again Lord Randall had proved himself to be a surprising man, she thought, as she climbed over the stile. He had revealed a concern for her welfare that she would not have expected by telling her of the short cut, and it was with this happy thought in mind that she walked back to the Grange.

CHAPTER SIX

When she had recovered from her initial surprise at being told she would be expected to join the boating-party, Sarah found herself looking forward to it. She could not remember the last time she had been to a social gathering, although she had frequently gone to parties and balls when she had lived in Derbyshire. Despite her mother's illness her father had always made sure she had time to enjoy herself, and had taken charge whenever Sarah was invited elsewhere. And now what a joy it was to be going into company again.

The weather, after a spell of rain the day before, did not disappoint them. The morning dawned bright, and by the afternoon it had set fair. Sarah's green sarsenet was newly washed and pressed, and her green kid slippers, a remnant of more prosperous days, were newly cleaned. She dressed carefully and then, putting on her straw hat, she went to collect the children.

The boys were in their study, eagerly waiting for her.

'I thought two o'clock would never come,' declared Preston as the three of them went to fetch Lucy.

'Me too,' said Fitzwilliam.

'I thought it was certain to rain,' said Lucy

as they went down to the terrace, where the guests were to assemble.

Lord Randall was already there, looking casual and relaxed. He was dressed in nankeen breeches, with snowy linen and a light coat, perfect for a summer's day. He turned and smiled when Sarah and the children stepped out on to the terrace.

Dominic, too, was already there, and the Reverend Mr Walker soon arrived.

'Oh! What a splendid idea! Splendid! So kind! So thoughtful! Such noble condescension!' he declared as he introduced himself to Lord Randall. 'I was only saying to Mother this morning, my lord, what a splendid idea it is. And how kind, how noble, of you to invite a humble clergyman! I am truly overwhelmed.'

Mr Walker's rotund face, bedewed with perspiration, was a picture of gratification.

'Not at all,' murmured James, hastily turning away as he caught Sarah's eye. The clergyman was undeniably comical, and he did not want to give way to his feelings of mirth.

Sarah, feeling as tempted to laugh as he did, took the children to examine an urn of flowers at the other end of the terrace until the rest of the guests arrived. Mr and Miss Wilberforce soon followed Mr Walker, Mr Wilberforce being a vague, thin gentleman with a wisp of grey hair, who was completely dominated by his battle-axe of a sister. With her ramrod back and her glinting eye, Miss Wilberforce evidently wore the trousers in their household. Mr Masterson was the last to arrive. He was a pleasant gentleman, courteous and polite; the sort of man any hostess would welcome as an addition to her party. He was still young enough to be considered eligible, but not so young that he might be liable to drink too much or be tempted to make a row.

'And may I present Miss Davenport,' said James, 'and her charges, Fitzwilliam, Preston and Lucy.'

Sarah was both surprised and touched by his tact. By introducing her in her own right he had set the tone for the afternoon, and made it clear that she was to be treated like any other guest.

Once everyone had arrived, they walked down to the lake.

The Watermead lake lay a good ten-minute walk from the house, and was large enough to provide an hour's walk all round. Water-lilies floated on the blue-green surface, and tall reeds grew round the banks. To one side was a landing-stage, and it was towards this that Lord Randall now led his party. Two boats were tied up, ready to take the guests on a trip across the water.

The first boat was to contain Sarah, Mr Walker, Miss Wilberforce and Mr Masterson, whilst the second was to contain James, Dominic, Mr Wilberforce and the children. This had pleased and delighted Sarah. It would do Lord Randall good to spend time with the children, and besides, she would find the afternoon much easier if she was not in too close proximity with him.

'Who ever would have thought it?' said Mr Walker as he sat down in the rowing-boat, his portly figure creaking as it moved, giving evidence of the corsets he wore beneath his black clothes. He settled himself across from Sarah and next to Miss Wilberforce. 'I'm sure I'd no more idea of being invited to such an illustrious gathering, with such agreeable company, than I had of being taken to the moon! My dear mother—who is so sorry she could not be present on account of her rheumatism—said to me only the other day, "Cedric. This is a signal honour".' His voice took on a grave and serious tone, as if to impress on his listeners how sensible he was of the honour conveyed by the invitation. ' "It is the greatest honour ever to befall our family," she said. "You must make sure you wear your flannel vest".'

At this mention of his undergarments, which perhaps accounted in part for his rotund figure as well as his heavy perspiration, Miss Wilberforce pursed her lips and unfurled her parasol with a great show of displeasure. She opened and closed it several times before finally holding it rigidly above her iron-grey head. She then turned away from the well-meaning clergyman and ostentatiously proceeded to admire the view.

The boat pulled away from the shore. It was rowed by two strong oarsmen who worked as labourers on the estate. Behind it the other boat, into which Lord Randall was helping the children, was waiting for Dominic and Mr Wilberforce to sit down before it followed the first.

'You will join me, I'm sure,' said the Reverend Mr Walker to his companions, undeterred by the fact that Miss Wilberforce had turned her back on him, 'when I say what a fine man our host is proving himself to be.'

'Lord Randall is a gentleman,' said Miss Wilberforce without, however, turning round.

'Indeed he is, dear lady! Indeed he is. A perfect gentleman. I'm sure I agree.'

Sitting opposite this odd couple in the pleasure boat, Sarah was forced to smile. The Reverend Mr Walker was trying so hard to please, and Miss Wilberforce—an ageing spinster—was determined he should not succeed. Taking pity on him Sarah asked, 'How long have you been in this part of Kent, Mr Walker? I understand you've only just arrived.'

The Reverend Mr Walker turned to her gratefully as the boat sculled over the water. He began to tell her all about the mingled worries and delights that filled his new life and Sarah listened attentively, making him feel more comfortable than he had felt all afternoon. For, although the invitation to Watermead Grange had been a feather in his cap, he had to admit that he had been rather out of his depth so far.

Sarah's attention, however, did not suit Miss Wilberforce. Before long she joined in the conversation.

'For if there is one thing I enjoy,' she declared when she had grown tired of being affronted by the mention of Mr Walker's vest, 'it is conversation.'

She soon dominated the proceedings, giving her advice—completely unasked for!—on every subject under the sun. Mr Masterson was told how to subdue foreign armies; Sarah was told how to turn her pupils into infant prodigies; and poor Mr Walker was given so much 'good advice' that he didn't know whether he was coming or going! And once she had finished with everyone's professional lives, Miss Wilberforce started on their personal lives.

'You should be ashamed of yourself,' she told Mr Walker. 'A man of your age should be married. It is up to you, as a man of the cloth, to set a good example.' A sudden thought struck her. 'In fact,' she said, 'you could do far worse than offer for Miss Davenport.'

Sarah's eyes opened wide at this impertinence. So far she had suffered Miss Wilberforce's interference politely, but this was going too far.

Poor Mr Walker was very alarmed and spluttered helplessly that he would be charmed . . . but . . .

'You must encourage him, Miss Davenport,' said Miss Wilberforce determinedly. 'Gentlemen always need a little encouragement at first.'

'I should not care to encourage anyone who is so happy being a bachelor,' replied Sarah. Mr Walker might be nonplussed, but she was fully equal to Miss Wilberforce's impertinence!

Mr Walker heaved a huge sigh of relief, and pulled an enormous handkerchief out of his pocket. 'That is just the way of it,' he blustered, casting a grateful look at Sarah. 'A bachelor! And so necessary to dear mother, or else offering for such an admirable young lady would make me the happiest of men!'

'Well!' declared Miss Wilberforce. 'I was only trying to be of service, I am sure.'

'And I thank you for it,' replied Sarah, too amused to be affronted by the ridiculous suggestion. 'But if and when I decide to marry, I am quite capable of choosing my own husband.'

'You? Choose?' Miss Wilberforce looked scandalized by Sarah's suggestion that a young lady might have a *choice*. 'My dear young lady, it is for the gentleman to choose.'

'And is the lady to have no say in the matter?' asked Sarah innocently.

Miss Wilberforce was not used to anyone standing up to her and was so surprised that she could not think of a cutting reply, so that she was reduced to being afffonted again. 'Well, really! I find this conversation most indelicate,' she declared. Which, as she had introduced the subject of matrimony in the first place, was a complete *volte face.*

But Sarah was not to be put out by Miss Wilberforce's displeasure, as Mr Walker had been, and replied coolly, 'I agree.'

'I have always thought how pleasant it is to be on the water when it is hot,' said Mr Masterson, changing the subject.

Mr Walker and Sarah were both glad to help him restore harmony in the boat, and fell to talking of other things. But Miss Wilberforce was determined not to let the subject drop until she had the last word.

'The lady,' she said forcefully, 'may say "yea" or "nay".'

'Just so,' said Mr Masterson politely.

He found Miss Wilberforce tiresome, but he was too much of a gentleman to show it. Therefore he made her a slight bow, with just an inclination of his head, before turning once again to Sarah. 'You are a good sailor, Miss Davenport,' he commented.

Sarah smiled. 'I hardly think the lake a test.'

'Perhaps not. But I'll warrant you would enjoy the open sea. Have you ever made a crossing?'

Sarah admitted that she had not, but she was interested to hear about his experiences of the Channel, and of the Atlantic, which he had crossed when he had been sent to fight in America some years before.

'Masterson seems to have a lot to say for himself,' commented Dominic in an aside to James, as there came a lull in the conversation in James's boat. 'He has been talking ever since his boat set off. He's given Miss Wilberforce a set-down, by the look of it, but he and Miss Davenport seem to be getting along famously.'

'Really? I hadn't noticed,' remarked James, wondering, a moment later, why he had told such a barefaced lie. Because throughout his conversation with Mr Wilberforce—a dithery old gentleman with a mania for collecting butterflies and moths—he had found his attention drifting again and again to Sarah.

She was looking particularly fresh and pretty in her sarsenet gown. The straw hat which completed her outfit suited the delicate oval of her face, and the green ribbon which was tied with a bow beneath her chin brought out the colour of her eyes. Their sea green seemed almost emerald today, and sparkled with a luminescence that roused the sleeping panther in him. It was a good thing he had sent her ahead in the other boat, or else he would have found it impossible to pay attention to anyone else. It was a pity, though, that he had not taken Masterson with him. Dominic could have travelled in the other boat, and would not have monopolized Miss Davenport.

'I dare say he's in love with her,' remarked Preston. He was in high spirits, having been allowed to take the oars for a while, and consequently overstepped the mark of politeness.

'Preston,' James cautioned him. He had relaxed considerably in his manner with the children, but he was still concerned to make sure they grew up with good manners.

'People don't fall in love in an afternoon, Preston,' Dominic explained. 'There's a lot more to it than that.'

'And anyway, it isn't manners for children to talk about a lady and a gentleman being in love,' Lucy informed him. She spoke with immense gravity, her arms folded across her chest, and sounded so comical, giving out advice on manners as though she had been an old lady of sixty instead of a little girl of six, that the tension was broken and they all laughed.

All except Mr Wilberforce, who was oblivious to the general conversation, and continued his own monologue on the subject of moths.

The boat went smoothly on its way across the lake. But James could not stop his eyes from drifting towards the other boat, and the figures of Mr Masterson and Miss Davenport.

They *did* seem to be getting on famously. And he happened to know for a fact that Masterson was looking for a wife.

For some reason he was not comfortable. He resettled himself in his seat, but instead of making him more comfortable it seemed to make him worse. He knew he should be paying more attention to Wilberforce, but his thoughts kept returning to the children's governess.

It would be a good match for her. Masterson was intelligent and good natured. He had no vices. He could provide Miss Davenport with a comfortable establishment and agreeable company. His rank was not too far above her own; for although Miss Davenport was a governess she was the daughter of a gentleman, and Masterson was nothing more than a squire. There was nothing, in short, to make it unsuitable. Then why did he find himself so hostile to the idea? If he could really have believed that Masterson was a Radical, working to overthrow the government, he would have felt justified in feeling hostile, but he did not seriously believe that Masterson was the person he was looking for. Masterson had answered all his leading questions openly when they had talked together on their way down to the lake, and James was convinced Masterson was what he appeared to be; a small landowner, newly returned from the wars, who wanted nothing more than to settle down and farm his few acres in peace.

'. . . The pride of my collection must be a moth I caught back in 1798. Or was it 1799?' droned on Mr Wilberforce, without the slightest idea that no one was paying him any attention.

So why was it, thought James, that, when the match would be so suitable, he could not bear the thought of Sarah in Masterson's arms?

* * *

Back on terra firma, later that afternoon James had an opportunity to talk to Mr Walker and Miss Wilberforce. He had not forgotten that the main purpose of the boating-party had been to talk to his new neighbours and try and discover, throughout the course of the conversation, whether they were of a Radical persuasion. It was easy enough to get them to talk. Mr Walker responded both gratefully and enthusiastically to his attention, and Miss Wilberforce was in her element, telling him how he should treat his servants and run his estate. It was somewhat with relief that he finally managed to extricate himself from the conversation, and found himself once more with Dominic.

The two men strolled beyond earshot of the rest of the company. Sarah was playing with the children down by the water's edge; Miss Wilberforce had returned to her brother; and the Reverend Mr Walker was telling the tolerant Mr Masterson all about his mother's many ailments.

'Have you discovered what you needed to know?' asked Dominic. 'Are any of these people Radicals?'

'It seems highly unlikely,' admitted James.

'I thought not,' said Dominic with a satisfied sigh.

'If they were down here to make trouble they would be cautious about what they said, but you're right, Dom. None of them seem like the people I'm looking for. Wilberforce is far too vague about everything except his moths. Besides, I've had enquiries made. He's a well-known amateur entomologist and has spent his life collecting insects.'

'And Miss Wilberforce?' asked Dominic.

James shook his head. 'She, too, passes scrutiny. Miss Wilberforce is interested in good works—in other words, in telling other people what to do. That kind of character doesn't go with being a Radical. The Radicals want to change the order of things. Miss Wilberforce wants them to stay the way they are.'

'So that she can boss and bully the lower orders to her heart's content,' said Dominic.

'Exactly. Which leaves Walker and Masterson. Walker may appear foolish on the surface, but he's a devout man and a good servant of the church. He would never encourage people to bloodshed. And Masterson . . .' He thought again of Masterson talking and laughing with Sarah, but pushed the image out of his mind. 'I've spoken to Masterson's commanding officer. He was a good soldier, and he is faithful to the crown.'

'And Miss Davenport?' asked Dominic.

James turned and looked at Sarah, who was collecting daisies with Lucy beside the lake. 'No,' he smiled. 'Miss Davenport is no Radical.' Beautiful, charming, and intelligent—yes. But a Radical agitator? No.

'Of course not,' said Dominic. 'If you ask me, it was all a mare's nest. Napoleon's safely imprisoned on Elba. He'll never escape. And the Radicals who want to make trouble over here—well, it's probably nothing more than hot air.'

James could have told Dom that he had that very morning received confirmation of the fact that a Radical group was operating in Kent, but he chose not to. Dominic's temperament was too open and trusting to harbour suspicion for long, and even if James had managed to convince his friend that the dangers they had spoken about were real it would serve no purpose. Dominic could do nothing more to help, and to know that the problem hadn't gone away would only worry him. So James kept what he knew to himself.

'Come on, Dom,' he said, clapping his friend on the arm. 'We've been away from the company long enough.'

They strolled back together. On reaching the others, Dominic's attention was claimed by Miss Wilberforce, who wanted his advice on hiring a groom, and James continued down to the water's edge. The boys had run off amongst the trees, and Lucy was busy adding to her pile of daisies. On the jetty, two of the labourers were putting coils of rope in the boats. Sarah, having examined a collection of fungi the boys had picked earlier, was rinsing her hands in the lake.

She looked so beautiful as she knelt there, letting her hands drift through the water, that he couldn't help stopping to look at her. The sunlight was falling across her hair, brightening it and making it shine. Several tendrils had fallen loose, and were being blown back and forth across her graceful neck.

She stood up, shaking the water from her hands. Turning, she saw him, and her breath caught in her throat. There was a look of such intensity flaring out of his black eyes that, as she met his gaze, everything else disappeared—the water's edge, the children, the labourers—everything except the two of them, standing there facing each other. And not facing each other as Lord Randall and governess, but facing each other as two equal human beings; as man and woman; Adam and

Eve; two beings whose minds cried out to each other in that one stretched moment, and whose bodies longed to be joined.

So strong was the attraction that Sarah stepped forward, drawn towards him as a needle is drawn to a magnet. James, in the grip of the same powerful attraction, strode towards her, not stopping until he stood so close to her that he could reach out and touch her. With only the smallest gap between them, the last bastion of conventionality, they stood facing each other, oblivious of everything else.

James fought with his desires. If he lifted his hand, if he pushed back the strand of hair that was blowing across her cheek, if he took her face in his hands, if he kissed her as he was hungry to do, he would destroy her reputation for ever.

He could not do it.

He must not do it.

But restraining himself was almost unbearable.

Sarah, tied to him by the charged atmosphere that surrounded them, and her own nameless desires, tried to break the spell that held them. If she could only move; speak; do something to shatter the unbearable tension; but her limbs were weak and her mouth was dry.

Release came in an unexpected form.

Lucy, with a handful of her precious daisies, brought them over to Sarah. 'Miss Davenport.

Miss Davenport!' she said.

The spell was broken. Sarah, relieved the danger was past and yet conscious of an unaccountable sinking sensation none the less, turned from James and gave her attention to the little girl. Gradually her heart began to steady its beat, and her legs began to regain their strength. The fluttering in her stomach subsided and she breathed more evenly, taking in the balmy summer air.

James, no less grateful for the interruption, however frustrating it was, strode over to the labourers. He loosened his cravat as he went. His shirt, his cravat, his breeches—all had become too tight during that one stretched moment by the side of the lake. Miss Davenport drove him to distraction. But she was his niece's governess, and as such she was under his care and protection. And besides, had he not already as good as proposed to Margaret Leatherhead? A young lady from an old and well-respected family? A meek, respectful, quiet and biddable beauty who would make him a perfect wife?

The idea of a perfect wife suddenly and unaccountably made him frown, as though there was something wrong with it. But that was surely ridiculous. What could be wrong with having a perfect wife?

Sarah took the daisies Lucy was holding out to her.

'You promised to show me how to make a

daisy-chain,' Lucy reminded her.

Sarah smiled and, kneeling down on the grass beside Lucy, proceeded to show her how to thread the daisies together. As Lucy added more and more daisies to the chain, it seemed to Sarah to be like the chain that bound her to Lord Randall; because there was no denying the strong physical attraction that bound them together—however dangerous that bond might be.

* * *

Sarah's feelings were firmly under control again by the time she walked back to the house. The guests had departed, leaving her alone with Lord Randall and the children.

'That was a lovely day,' said Lucy, taking Sarah's hand as they made their way across the smooth green lawn to the Grange.

'Rather!' said Preston, tired but happy.

'Perfect!' declared Fitzwilliam grandly.

'I want to thank you for today,' said Lord Randall, detaining Sarah as the children ran into the house. 'It was an excellent idea for the children to join us. I hadn't realized how much they would learn from mixing with adults, or how much they would learn in other ways besides. Fitzwilliam made a good stab at rowing, and so did Preston. I'd forgotten that I could already handle a boat at their age.'

'It would be good for them to learn,' said

Sarah.

He considered. 'They can both swim—yes. It's something they should be able to do. I'll arrange for it.'

Sarah was disappointed that he had not thought of teaching the boys himself, but still, if he had realized there was more to life than the schoolroom then she was pleased. She couldn't hope for everything at once. Lord Randall's manner towards the children had relaxed greatly since his arrival at the Grange and she realized that it could not have been easy for him to make such a big adjustment in such a short space of time.

After all, he had been giving orders to hundreds of seasoned men just a few short months before.

'And you didn't think Lucy was too young?' she asked, looking up at him with a sudden unaccountable shyness. Although the strange force that had bound them together was gone, there was an undeniable attraction between them and even now she was aware of him in a way she had never been aware of a man before.

'Lucy surprised me. She's very sensible for a child so young. And good at making daisy-chains,' he said, a smile softening his face as his eyes dropped to the daisy-chain adorning Sarah's slender wrist.

Sarah lifted her hand and the chain slid further up her arm.

As he watched it glide over her golden skin, raising the downy hairs, James felt his body stir again. Realizing that the situation was becoming dangerous, realizing that the temptation she unknowingly offered him simply by being herself was becoming too much for him to bear, he made her a bow, saying, 'I must not detain you,' and strode off towards the stables.

And Sarah, wishing she knew not what, inclined her head and followed the children into the house.

* * *

After all the excitement of the afternoon, Sarah was happy to sit and hem a handkerchief that evening in her room. The mellow evening light was casting a warm glow over the gardens, and, sitting on the window seat, Sarah could both hem her handkerchief and make the most of the view. She had almost finished when there was a knock at the door and Mrs Smith, the housekeeper, entered.

'Excuse me for bothering you,' she said, seeing that Sarah was busy, 'but I just wanted to make sure that everything went well this afternoon. Lord Randall is in the stables, and I don't want to disturb him.'

'Yes, it was very well arranged. The refreshments you sent down to the lake were enjoyed by everyone.'

Mrs Smith looked pleased. 'Oh, good. I must say it's a pleasure to have some life about the Grange again,' she said. 'And how good it is to see Mr Dominic looking so happy again—although, Mr Transom I should call him. Many's the time I've seen him and the master rowing on the lake. When they were boys, they always used to play together. It was such a pity when there was all that business about Miss Yardley, but then, it's good to see it's all blown over now.' She did not usually spend her time in gossip, but the boating-party had put something of a strain on the household, which had got out of the way of arranging entertainments, and she was in a rare mood to talk. 'I did think for a while after Lord Randall told Mr Transom he couldn't marry Miss Yardley he'd never be happy again.'

Sarah looked up from her stitching in surprise. It was the first time she had heard of Miss Yardley.

'Not but I'm sure Lord Randall was right,' said Mrs Smith hastily. It was not her custom to talk about Lord Randall, his private life being none of her affair, and she did not allow the servants to gossip about him either. But she had let the words out in an unguarded moment and she wanted to make sure that Sarah did not think she was implying any criticism of him.

Sarah's attention, however, was caught. She had taken to Dominic, who had been good company, and asked in surprise, 'But surely Mr Transom doesn't allow Lord Randall to run his life?'

'I don't know about running his life, but his lordship always helps his friend when he's in a scrape.'

'I hardly think the desire to get married can be considered a scrape!' Sarah smiled.

Mrs Smith pursed her lips. 'That depends on who the intended is,' she replied. She didn't want Sarah to blame Lord Randall in any way: Lord Randall, to Mrs Smith's way of thinking, was beyond reproach. 'Miss Yardley is a very vulgar young woman.' Then, remembering that she had never met the young woman, she justified her comment by adding, 'One of the new families. No pedigree. And a father in trade.'

'Hardly a reason for calling her vulgar,' returned Sarah, feeling that Lord Randall had used his friend very ill. 'The poor young lady can't help it if she doesn't have a pedigree.'

'She wasn't poor,' said Mrs Smith, misunderstanding Sarah's remark. She shook her head. 'No. In fact Miss Yardley was very wealthy by all accounts, with a dowry of thirty thousand pounds. But quite beneath Mr Transom, whose mother was related to a marquis, no less.'

'And did Mr Transom love her?' Sarah asked, laying her handkerchief to one side.

'Oh, yes. His face lit up whenever he spoke

about her. She was a charming young lady; pretty, lovely in every way. But not fit for Mr Transom, of course, and his lordship told him so. "Unequal marriages never work," his lordship said. I heard it from Mr Transom himself.'

'But why did Mr Transom not tell him to mind his own business?' demanded Sarah.

'He couldn't do that!' Mrs Smith was shocked.

'Why ever not? If he loved Miss Yardley he had no business abandoning her on the say-so of his friend.'

'Ah, but Mr Transom has always been the weaker of the two,' said Mrs Smith with a shake of her head.

'Then it is wrong of Lord Randall to have taken advantage of him,' declared Sarah.

'Who knows? It was probably a good thing.'

'A good thing to tell Mr Transom he can't marry a charming young lady, simply because she isn't his equal in birth?' demanded Sarah. 'No, indeed. It was wrong of him. Very wrong. And it was foolish of Mr Transom to let him.'

'Still, Mr Transom seems happy enough now,' said Mrs Smith, returning to her earlier comments. 'And a good thing, too. Never a better gentleman has there been than Mr Transom—unless it is the master.'

As to that, Sarah thought, picking up her handkerchief as Mrs Smith left the room and stabbing it with her needle, we will have to disagree.

But why should it matter to her that Lord Randall disapproved of unequal marriages? she asked herself.

She was uncomfortably aware of the answer to that question, but no good could come of allowing her feelings to follow that path, so taking up her needle again she devoted herself to finishing her handkerchief and, with a determined effort, pushed all other thoughts out of her mind.

CHAPTER SEVEN

It was evening, a few days after the boating-party. Sarah was sitting beneath a spreading elm in the middle of the lawn behind the house. She had just handed the children over to Lucy's nurse as she did every evening at Lucy's bedtime, the boys passing into the nurse's care at that time until they, too, were ready for bed. The air was still and balmy. It was a perfect evening, and Sarah's occupation was perfect for it. She was reading *Childe Harold's Pilgrimage*, the work by Byron that had so captured the imagination of the fashionable world and which Lord Randall had lent her.

'It must be a good book, miss.'

The words took Sarah by surprise, as she

had not noticed that Sam, the gardener's boy, was working near by.

'It is,' said Sarah. She had been finding it difficult to concentrate, her mind wandering back to the boating afternoon and to the intense moment by the lake she had shared with her enigmatic employer; so that she was glad to put the book down for a few minutes and talk to Sam.

'Seen you reading it for ages now, miss. Must take a deal of reading, a book like that.'

Sarah smiled. 'Reading's like everything else. It gets easier with practice.'

Sam laughed. 'That's what the parson used to say. Old Mr Merriweather. Him that was here before Walker. Lives down by the sea now, in one of Farbey's cottages. "It only takes practice, Sam," he used to say. And my dad said so too. But my dad never could learn to read, miss, all the same.'

'Now then, boy,' came a stern voice behind them. 'Don't you go bothering Miss Davenport. She ain't got time for the likes o' you.'

It was Todd, the head gardener.

Sam gave a guilty start and picked up his hoe, which he had been leaning on whilst he talked to Sarah.

'His lordship wants those flower-beds seeing to by tonight, young Sam, not by next Christmas.'

Sam, suitably chastened, returned to work.

'Sorry if he was bothering you, miss,' said Todd. To his mind, young under-gardeners had no business talking to educated young misses.

'He wasn't,' Sarah assured him with a smile.

'Then no harm done.'

He tugged his forelock and moved away, leaving Sarah to read on in peace. The poetry was both beautiful and melancholy, and Sarah felt closer to Lord Randall as she read it, knowing they both enjoyed Byron's verse.

It was still early but, having finished the *Pilgrimage*, Sarah decided to go inside. She had one or two pieces of mending to do and wanted to get them done before the light disappeared. She went into the house through the side entrance, this being the nearest door to her, and then went leisurely up the back stairs to her room.

As she walked along the corridor she was surprised to see that the door to her room was open. She frowned. The maids saw to the cleaning before lunch, and there was no reason for anyone else to be there. Quickening her step, she reached the open door to see Nelly, one of the under-housemaids, standing by her window.

'What are you doing in here?' asked Sarah curiously, as she set down her book.

Nelly turned round with a start. She was a plain girl, with oversized hands and feet, and she blushed guiltily at Sarah's question.

'What are you doing in here?' repeated Sarah more sternly.

She had been expecting Nelly to say that she had been sent with a message from Mrs Smith, or some other such thing, but Nelly's face told Sarah there wasn't an innocent explanation for her presence in the room.

'I . . . I forgot something,' said Nelly.

It was an obvious lie. Sarah thought for a moment before asking, 'What did you forget?'

'The . . . my . . . the . . . that is, the duster. Yes, that's what it was,' said Nelly, fingering her apron awkwardly. 'The feather duster.'

'And did you find it?' enquired Sarah. It was obvious by now that Nelly was lying, but having no way of proving it Sarah went along with the pretence.

'Why, no, miss,' blustered Nelly. 'I can't have left it here after all.'

'Then you had better go and look for it elsewhere,' remarked Sarah.

Nelly threw her a sullen look, but replied simply, 'Yes, miss,' before hurrying out of the room.

Now what was all that about? wondered Sarah.

She walked over to the window and opened it. A light breeze blew across her cheek, and the scent of roses drifted up from below. What had Nelly been looking at? she wondered. But she did not have to wonder for long. Walking away from the house, his hands thrust into the pockets of his breeches, was an unmistakable figure. It was Mr Haversage.

Sarah gave a sigh.

So Nelly has a crush on Mr Haversage, too, she thought. Along with every other maid in the building! Nelly must have caught sight of him in the rose-gardens and decided that Sarah's room would be an excellent spot from which to moon over him.

Well, at least the mystery was solved.

She left the window open and was just going over to the washstand when something white and fluttering caught her eye, something that had fallen down the back of one of the cushions that were comfortably arranged on the window seat. Curious, she pulled it out from behind the cushion. As soon as she realized what it was her eyes went to the door, through which Nelly had just departed. The item was a letter; one of the letters Sarah's brother had written to her during her stay at the Grange.

She picked it up and turned it between her fingers, her lips pursed. She never left her brother's letters lying about. She always put them away in her desk.

Could she have forgotten to put this one away? She didn't think so. Then could Nelly have taken the letter out of her desk?

It was possible. But why should she? What possible interest could Nelly have in Sarah's letters? And why would she have risked instant dismissal—for Sarah knew Lord Randall well enough to know that he would not tolerate dishonesty—to look at a letter which could have no possible interest for her?

Crossing the room, Sarah put the letter back in her desk. She closed the top of the desk but then hesitated before leaving it. She did not know why Nelly had been prying and she was uncomfortable with the thought that the maid might try the same thing again. She did not want to have Nelly dismissed—the girl came from a poor family and Sarah understood the hardships of poverty only too well—but she did not want the same thing to happen again. She could talk to Nelly herself, but there was no guarantee the girl would listen to a lecture from her.

But Nelly would listen to Mrs Smith.

After thinking the matter over, Sarah decided to tell the housekeeper what had happened. The maids were Mrs Smith's responsibility and a stern word from her should be enough to stop Nelly overstepping the mark again.

Sarah left her room and made her way along the passage to the housekeeper's room. She was just passing the turning to the picture gallery, which was situated in the west wing of the house, when she heard the sound of Preston's voice. She stopped, surprised: Preston should surely be in bed.

But no. She had not stayed out by the lake

as long as usual tonight, which was why Nelly had not expected to be discovered, and there were still ten minutes or so before the nurse would send Preston to bed.

She was about to go on but she was surprised to hear that Preston was talking to Lord Randall, and a minute later she realized that he was excitedly telling Lord Randall about a small concert the children were preparing for the house-party, as a treat for the guests.

She smiled. It had been Fitzwilliam's idea to arrange a concert, and one she had been glad to encourage. The children had set to with a will, Lucy learning a pretty little song called *The Waterfall*, and the two boys learning passages from Milton and Shakespeare. Sarah had enjoyed helping them to learn the music and poetry with which to entertain their father's guests.

'. . . been practising a speech for the concert,' Preston was saying enthusiastically.

A month ago, Preston would not have dared speak to Lord Randall so confidently and openly, and Sarah felt a real sense of satisfaction at the difference the last few weeks had made.

But her sense of satisfaction turned to surprise a minute later as she heard Lord Randall's reply.

'That's impossible, Preston. The house-party isn't for children. It's for adult guests.'

'But . . .' Preston began to protest. His tone was bewildered.

Sarah, too, felt bewildered as she overheard what was being said.

'No arguments,' said Lord Randall with authority.

Impossible man! thought Sarah, angry at Lord Randall's high-handed attitude and full of sympathy for the disappointment that dripped from Preston's every word. She had thought that Lord Randall's attitude to the children had really improved, but, if the present conversation was anything to go by, it hadn't changed a bit.

'I've been practising for weeks, sir,' protested Preston. 'And so has—'

'Preston,' said Lord Randall firmly. 'I said "no". Now go to your room. It is high time you were in bed.'

He knew he was being hard on the boy, but he had had a long day. One of the tenant farmers had come to him with news of poachers; there had been trouble with the irrigation system for the low-lying fields; he was no nearer to discovering the identity of the Radicals, a problem which was constantly on his mind; and on top of everything else, one of his favourite mares had been taken ill with no one knowing why. Even the horse-doctor had been puzzled, and although the man had given the mare a noxious-smelling potion he had held out little hope of its success. So that Lord

Randall was troubled; and he did not want to talk to Preston about a concert he had never heard of until he was in a better mood.

Preston remained mutinous, and in exasperation Lord Randall said, 'Did you hear me, Preston?'

At this, Sarah decided to step in and take a hand. She had worked hard over the last few weeks to give the children some sort of confidence, and she was not going to have that work ruined by Lord Randall in a single night.

As she turned the corner she saw Preston standing mutinously in front of Lord Randall. The boy wrestled with himself for a moment, and then said, 'Yes, sir,' from between his gritted teeth.

As she entered the picture-gallery she was just in time to see Preston running out of the door at the far end. His shoulders were drooping and he was clearly much upset.

'There was no need to speak to Preston like that,' she said.

'Miss Davenport!' Lord Randall turned towards her with a start. He had been so engrossed in his thoughts that he had not heard her enter the long picture-gallery.

'You could have let him down gently,' she said accusingly. 'There was no need for you to be so hard.'

Lord Randall's brow darkened. He had just been thinking exactly the same thing. But in his troubled state of mind he could not bring himself to admit it.

'Preston has spent weeks rehearsing a speech from *A Midsummer Night's Dream*,' went on Sarah. 'He has worked and worked at the difficult language and he has done it because he wants to make you proud of him. And Fitzwilliam and Lucy want to make you proud of them, too. They have been rehearsing a selection of music and poetry so that they can put on an entertainment for your guests.'

'They weren't asked to put on an entertainment,' said Lord Randall irritably.

'And what has that to do with it?' Sarah challenged him. 'Are they never to show any initiative? Are they never to think of anything for themselves? Are they never to try and make you proud of them? Any other man would be delighted to have such fine children'—here Lord Randall's expression changed, but Sarah was in full flow and failed to notice it—'but no matter how hard they try, it is simply impossible for them to please you. Don't you know how important it is for them to have their father's approval? Don't you—'

'You think I'm their father,' said Lord Randall. His voice was flat.

'—know how important it is,' continued Sarah, who was so determined to speak that she did not take in what he had said, 'for them to have someone to model themselves on, in particular Fitzwilliam and . . .'

Her voice trailed off and a look of confusion crossed her face as his words sank in.

'You think I'm their father, don't you?' he asked.

Sarah looked at him uncertainly. There was a strange expression on his face, but whether it was pain or anger or merely surprise she could not tell.

She suddenly felt unsure of herself. 'I . . . Yes . . .' She spoke hesitantly. 'That is . . . aren't you?'

'I should have told you, but I thought you knew. I never expected . . .' He stopped, his coal-black eyes looking directly into Sarah's own. Then he ran his hand through his black hair. 'No. I am not the children's father,' he began again, his voice firm and steady. 'I have tried to care for them as their father would have done, but the children are not mine.'

'Not . . .? Not your children?' asked Sarah, scarcely able to take it in. She was having to adjust rapidly to a completely unexpected development, and her confusion showed plainly on her face.

'No.'

All the strength was ebbing out of her, and her legs were beginning to feel weak. It was so sudden, and it had come as a shock. For weeks she had believed she was teaching Lord Randall's children. She had been judging him to be a stern and remote father; and now she discovered he was not their father at all. It demanded a complete change in her attitude, and that could not be accomplished all at once.

'But I thought . . . that is, Lady Templeton said . . .'

But as she spoke, she realized that Lady Templeton had never said that the children were the sons and daughters of her nephew. She had referred to them either as 'my great-niece' or 'my great-nephews', or simply as 'the children'. It was Sarah herself who, hearing Lady Templeton refer to Lord Randall as 'my nephew' and the children as 'my great-nephews' or 'my great-niece', had made that assumption. But hadn't Mr Haversage confirmed it, almost as soon as Lord Randall had returned to the Grange? Yes. She distinctly remembered talking to him about Lord Randall's children and remembered the way he had gone along with it. He had deliberately misled her. She now realized he really was devious and underhand. And he had rejoiced, no doubt, in making trouble for Sarah, in revenge for the way she had rebuffed his unwanted advances.

'I—I have made a fool of myself,' she said. A flush spread over her cheeks. She remembered all the times she had argued with Lord Randall, thinking he was the children's father, and those arguments now seemed out of place. It was one thing to challenge a strict parent; quite another to criticize a man who, unused to children, was doing his best for his wards.

She spoke in such a heartfelt way that Lord Randall found it totally disarming. He saw that underneath her determined surface Sarah was vulnerable. She was no longer the termagant who had confronted him on the stairs at their first meeting, or the strong character who had argued with him over so many aspects of the children's life. She was instead a young—and at that moment she seemed a very young—lady, who had coped admirably with all the demands placed on her, and not only coped, but triumphed. She had helped three lonely, uncertain children become happy and confident individuals.

And she had helped him. She had helped him to discover a new side to life, one he had never known existed until he had met her. He stood looking down at her with a look composed of admiration and unmistakable tenderness.

'No. Not a fool. Mistaken, yes. Rash—of course. But a fool? Never.' He spoke gently, all his earlier ill humour forgotten.

Her flush had subsided and she was looking pale. He pulled forward an elegant chair, of which there were any number lining the walls of the gallery, and said, 'You had better sit down.'

'I just assumed . . .' said Sarah miserably.

'It was a natural assumption to make. I should have told you.'

Sarah shook her head. 'No. You are my employer. You are the master here. You don't have to explain yourself in any way.'

A smile appeared at the corner of his lips. 'Except to explain why I wouldn't let the children play; why I wouldn't let them join the boating party; why I wouldn't allow them to arrange a concert for my guests . . .'

Sarah did not see his smile because her head was bowed, and with each fresh reminder of her outspokenness she felt a weight settling more and more heavily on her shoulders. At last she raised her eyes to his, searching for the words that would let her apologize for her tongue, which so often ran away with her; only to see by his smile that he was gently teasing her.

The weight on her shoulders began to lift.

Still, she knew she had not been an ideal governess, and said ruefully, 'I had no right to do anything of the kind.'

He surprised her by saying, 'You had every right. And I'm glad you did. I was mistaken, Sarah'—he spoke her name without noticing, so natural did it seem—'on each of those occasions. Particularly just now. I was harsh with Preston. I didn't mean to be, but I have a lot on my mind at the moment, and I have so little experience of children that I still forget from time to time how easily their feelings can be hurt. Which is why, although you have been a thorn in my side at times, I have been grateful to you for telling me where I have been going wrong. I never mean to be unkind, but I am used to dealing with soldiers—hardened men—not children who haven't left the schoolroom. I am getting better at understanding them, but I still have a lot to learn.'

Sarah sighed. She understood. 'But if they are not your children . . .' she began hesitantly.

'Whose are they?'

She nodded.

He pulled another chair forward. This time it was for himself. He sat down opposite her, so that he could look at her, and she at him.

'They are my nephews and niece, the children of my younger brother, Thomas.'

Sarah nodded. 'That explains it.'

'Explains what?' Lord Randall was curious.

'It explains why the children never call you "Father". Although they don't call you "Uncle" either,' she added thoughtfully. Which was not really surprising, she realized, as they hardly ever talked about Lord Randall at all. She had found it strange at first, but now she was beginning to realize why. It was because he had been away for so long that he had been only a shadowy figure in their lives, and therefore not someone they talked or even thought about.

He looked surprised. 'I never thought about what the children should call me. I have been in the army for most of my adult life, and when

I was on leave I spent my time in London and not in Kent, so that I very rarely saw them. They had their father and mother to look after them, and a doting grandfather, so that they did not need their uncle. It was not until Thomas and Caroline, his wife, were killed a few years ago in a carriage accident that the children were orphaned.'

'I'm sorry,' said Sarah. Her voice showed her genuine concern.

'It was a tragedy,' he acknowledged. 'The children became my father's wards, but when he died shortly afterwards they became mine. Fortunately, Napoleon had at last been defeated, and I was free to come home to look after the estate.' He paused. 'And the children.'

'Then you have hardly seen them,' said Sarah. She understood at last why Lord Randall was so unused to them.

'I did my best. The boys had excellent tutors—Caroline survived the accident by a few days and made me promise I would not send them away to school. Lucy had a governess and a nurse. A whole string of governesses!' he admitted. And then added, 'But never one who cared for her as you have done. And never one who told me how I, too, should care for them.'

'I never doubted that you cared for them. I just wondered why you didn't show it.'

'I didn't know how to.' He gave a rueful smile. 'It is a lot more difficult than I had supposed. But I'm learning,' he said. 'And that's thanks to you.'

'I never knew . . .'

'How could you? Lady Templeton neglected to explain the situation to you, and the rest of the household never corrected your mistake because they never realized you had made one.'

And Mr Haversage deliberately misled me, thought Sarah, but did not say so out loud.

They did not speak for some minutes. It was all so new and so unexpected that Sarah was having difficulty taking it in. Because it had changed something. She did not know quite how or what, but somewhere inside her it had changed her. And it had changed her attitude to the darkly handsome man who was so close to her.

So close . . .

She felt a shiver wash over her. She did not know what was causing it; only that it had everything to do with the man in front of her, and absolutely nothing to do with being cold.

He reached out his hand.

She looked up, eyes wide, as he stroked her face, brushing his fingers over her cheekbone and down to her lips. She trembled, and he bent towards her. Her lips half-parted and she closed her eyes. She could feel the warmth of his breath and smell the musky scent of him, a mixture of leather and stables and sweet cologne. The sensation of his nearness was like nothing she had ever experienced before. It was so all-consuming it drove everything else out of her mind . . . until the sound of footsteps forced their way into her consciousness.

He heard them, too, and drew back. Someone was approaching the gallery.

He turned away in frustration, as Sarah tried to gather her thoughts, and a minute later Hodgess appeared.

'Begging your pardon, my lord,' said Hodgess discreetly, 'but the head groom says you are needed urgently in the stables.'

Lord Randall gave a long, shuddering sigh. 'Thank you, Hodgess,' he said, turning round again. 'Tell Dixon I will be there at once.' He turned to Sarah, half relieved that he had been prevented from kissing her, and half unbearably frustrated. 'I have to leave you.'

She swallowed, then nodded. She knew he had to go. Knew, too, that it was better he did. Because if he stayed she did not know what might happen.

For a moment he looked as if he might change his mind and stay. But then the gentler side of his nature that had appeared at the sight of Sarah's obvious distress faded, to be replaced by his habitual lordly bearing.

'Miss Davenport has had something of a shock,' he said to Hodgess. 'Bring her a brandy—'

'No,' said Sarah, standing up. 'That is, I'm

quite all right.'

'A brandy, Hodgess,' he said, overriding her. 'And make sure she drinks it.'

'Yes, my lord. Very good, my lord,' replied Hodgess imperturbably.

James strode out of the gallery. Hodgess followed. Leaving Sarah alone, trying to make sense of what had happened to her.

Had Lord Randall really been about to kiss her? she wondered. No. She must have imagined it. She had no experience of such things after all; she must have made a mistake. Lord Randall would never kiss a governess. He had been about to comfort her, that was all.

She stood up, and to take her mind off the incident she decided to take a turn around the gallery. It was full of landscapes and portraits. Different views of the Grange predominated along the near wall, together with a number of hunting scenes, whilst portraits of the family occupied the far wall. There hung all Lord Randall's ancestors, the Earl and Countess who had founded the dynasty in the seventeenth century together with all their descendants. All people who had once lived and loved at the Grange.

She stopped in front of the most recent portraits, looking at a charming family grouping. It was of Lord and Lady Randall, together with two people Sarah now guessed to be Thomas and Caroline, Lord Randall's brother and sister-in-law. In front of them were the three children: Fitzwilliam, Preston and Lucy. They had been much younger when the portrait was painted, but they were still easy to recognize.

So Lord Randall is not their father, mused Sarah.

And Lady Randall, it followed, had not been their mother.

Sarah recalled Mrs Smith telling her, in a rare moment of volubility, that Lady Randall had died of a fever five years before, and this knowledge had intensified Sarah's belief that the children were his. If Lord Randall had been a bachelor instead of a widower she would have quickly discovered her mistake.

But Lord Randall's state, married or unmarried, was no concern of hers, she reminded herself firmly, and passed on to the next portrait, occupying herself by tracing the family features until Hodgess returned. As she sipped the—horrible!—brandy James had ordered for her she found herself wondering what Hodgess would make of finding her alone with his master in the picture-gallery. But she had no need to be concerned. Hodgess was an old and trusted retainer. Like Mrs Smith, he thought that everything Lord Randall did was automatically right.

*   *   *

It was a long night. Lord Randall spent most

of it in the stables with the sick mare, only leaving there towards dawn when the animal was showing signs of recovery. He slept late and afterwards, having seen that the mare was continuing to improve, rode out to the furthest reaches of his estate. Once there, in the peace and solitude of the beautiful landscape, he knew he would not be disturbed.

And he felt in need of peace and solitude, because for the first time in his life he was experiencing feelings he could not understand. And those feelings were centred around Miss Davenport, the children's governess.

His first response to her had been his normal one: he had been proud, arrogant and unconcerned. But even then she had stirred something in him, something he had not acknowledged until later, when he had had to admit to himself that she was a most unusual governess. His next response had been a purely physical one. Even so, if his feelings had ended there he could with difficulty have controlled them; after the look that had been surprised out of him by the lake he had kept a tight rein on himself and, knowing that he was so strongly attracted to her, he had made sure they did not meet too often. But their encounter in the picture-gallery had aroused new feelings in him, and ones he was less sure of controlling. She had been so vulnerable when she had learnt of her mistake about the children that he had discovered a new side of himself, a tender side he had not even known was there. He had wanted to help her, to make things easier for her. And that was something he had never felt about any woman. As he had never felt admiration or respect for a woman before he had met Sarah.

In the midst of many feelings that were uncertain, one thing was crystal-clear. He could not remain in the same house as her without his feelings developing further. And as he was not prepared for this to happen—as he was not prepared to find that his feelings for a governess were beyond his control—it would be better for him to remove himself from the Grange and return to London right away.

Just for a moment he wondered whether . . . but no.

Hadn't he saved Dom from making a similar mistake?

But that was because Miss Yardley had been Dom's inferior in every way, not just in the matter of birth. She had been vulgar and ignorant. Whereas Sarah . . .

He cut off the thought before it could flower. He had gone too far in the matter of Miss Leatherhead to pull back. Although he had not yet made her an offer he had paid her marked attention throughout the Season and if he did not propose it would be seen as a slight. She did not deserve that; particularly as it would jeopardize her chances of making a good match elsewhere.

No. He must stick to his original plan. He must go to London.

He had been meaning to go before the house-party anyway, as he needed to talk to the general about the Radical problem, and to see if any more clues to the agent's identity had been discovered. He would simply bring his journey forward by a few days.

A week in the capital, he told himself spent amongst the most highly regarded members of the *ton*, would soon remind him of his place in the world. And on his return he would be able to see Miss Davenport for what she truly was: the governess of his little niece, and nothing else.

But even as he thought it, he knew, deep down, that he was deceiving himself.

CHAPTER EIGHT

It was wet. The summer sunshine had broken at last, giving way to a day of storm-clouds and rain. Sarah was sitting with the children in the schoolroom, where Lucy was engaged in working a sampler whilst the boys were occupied with their Latin prep.

'But are you *sure*?' broke out Preston for what seemed like the hundredth time, looking up from his work.

'Yes, Preston, quite sure. Your uncle'—now

that she knew the truth about Lord Randall's relationship to the children she was determined to cement it by referring to him as 'your uncle'—'your uncle left instructions for you to continue practising your concert, so that you will be able to entertain his guests.'

Preston shook his head with a worried frown. 'But he seemed so *certain* that we weren't allowed to meet his guests. He said the house-party was for adults.'

'Your uncle was tired,' Sarah explained. 'He didn't mean to be so harsh with you, but he had had a difficult day, and on top of that one of his favourite mares was ill. He was bad-tempered and out of sorts, and that's why he said you were not allowed to meet his guests. But once he had had a chance to think it over he realized what a good idea it would be for you to put on an entertainment, and he left me a letter telling me to make sure that you were word-perfect by the time he returned.'

'I'm already word-perfect,' said Fitzwilliam, who had been spending every spare minute learning his passage from Milton. 'I know my speech inside out and upside down and back to front.'

'And I'm note-perfect—at least, nearly,' admitted Lucy truthfully.

'But he seemed so *sure*,' said Preston again.

'Oh, come off it Preston,' said Fitzwilliam loftily. 'You're just trying to make yourself important by going on about it. Miss

Davenport's told us a hundred times we can do the concert. And if Miss Davenport says it, then it's good enough for me!'

Sarah was forced to smile. Fitzwilliam had become so much more confident over the last few weeks. He had also become much more used to mixing with the stable hands, and the phrase 'If Miss Davenport says it, then it's good enough for me!' was an almost exact copy of Reuben's phrase, 'If the master says it, then it's good enough for me!'

Though quite what 'the master' would think of his nephew picking up words and phrases from the stable lads Sarah dreaded to think!

It had come as a surprise to her to discover that he had left for London, but although she had thought it odd, she found that she was nevertheless secretly relieved. Her feelings towards her employer had become increasingly confused and it would not do for her to let those feelings run away with her. He was an earl and she was a governess; he was her master and she was little more than his servant. And besides, there were rumours floating round the village that he was about to propose to Miss Margaret Leatherhead—an eminently suitable young lady who came from an old and well-connected family.

No. She must not let her feelings run away with her.

It was not as though she was in love with him.

True, he was the most devastatingly attractive man she had ever seen, and true, he made her aware, for the first time in her life, that she was a woman, and he a man, but that was not love, she told herself. Nor was the rapport they shared which made everything seem more interesting when she was with him. It was respect, understanding, attraction, esteem, she told herself, but not love.

'Did he *really* say we could have our concert?' asked Lucy, seeking one last reassurance from Sarah.

'Yes,' said Sarah, giving the little girl a hug. 'And now, if you're still not quite note-perfect, I suggest that we practise your song whilst the boys get on with their Latin verse.'

The two boys pulled a face.

'Oh, well,' said Preston, 'I'd rather do it here with you than with old—I mean, Mr Haversage.'

'That's no way to talk about your tutor,' said Sarah firmly. She knew the boys didn't like Mr Haversage, but she was not prepared to encourage them in their dislike for a man who, although she did not like him herself, was good at his job.

'Even so,' said Preston, with a burst of the high spirits Sarah had known him to be capable of, 'I'm glad Mr Haversage isn't here. Only because,' he went on with a change of tone as he saw Sarah's warning face, 'only because I don't want him to come back to work until he has had a good holiday.'

'I know *exactly* what you meant,' said Sarah sternly, and Preston, with one look at her unrelenting face, decided he had better drop his barbed comments about his tutor and pay attention to his work instead.

But although she had treated Preston sternly, Sarah could not help agreeing with the boy, and thinking that she, too, was not sorry that Mr Haversage was taking his annual leave.

The schoolroom was a much pleasanter place without him.

* * *

'Mrs Smith's compliments, miss, and here's a picnic for you to take and have as your lunch.'

Martha spoke respectfully as she handed Sarah a small wicker basket, and bobbed a curtsy as she did so. 'It's a long way to the ruins, so Mrs Smith says,' continued Martha. 'You'll be wanting something to eat when you get there.'

'Thank you, Martha,' said Sarah, taking the basket.

The leave at Watermead Grange was generous, and it was time for Sarah's day off. The weather was good and she intended to explore the ruins Mr Haversage had told her about some weeks earlier. She had not liked to follow his suggestion then in case he had taken it into his head to go with her, but now that he was safely on holiday she decided to go and see them.

Martha bobbed another curtsy, and after she had gone Sarah put the finishing touches to her *toilette.* She had trimmed her hat with the primrose ribbon and was wearing her yellow muslin gown. It was surprising what a difference her ribbons made to her outfits. By matching the colours she had almost managed to make them look *chic*. Almost, but not quite, she thought with a rueful smile as she looked in the cheval-glass. Because no matter how new her straw hat, or how bright her ribbon, her gowns were still unmistakably shabby and old. But with her next month's wages . . .

With her head happily full of the fabrics she hoped to buy in the future and turn into new gowns she set out at last for the ruins.

The walk was enjoyable, but when she arrived Sarah was surprised to find that the ruins were nothing more than a large tumbled-down house. From the way Mr Haversage had talked about them she had been expecting a ruined abbey or some such thing. Still, she spent an interesting half-hour walking amidst the ruins of the house, imagining the people who had lived there and picturing in her mind's eye what the house must have looked like when it was standing. After which she settled herself down in the shade of one of the more complete walls and opened her picnic hamper.

Mrs Smith had packed her a mouth-watering selection of pastries, including a chicken pasty and a small venison pie. There was also half a loaf of bread, a piece of ripe cheese, an assortment of fruit and some lemonade.

As Sarah ate, she felt deeply relaxed. The birds were singing and a gleam of sun showed through the clouds, brightening the otherwise dull day.

And after lunch, she thought to herself, I will explore further afield before going back to the Grange.

She ate her picnic with enjoyment and then, when she had finished, she stood up and brushed the crumbs from her muslin dress. She was just about to put on her straw hat, which she had laid aside before she had started to eat, when she had the strangest feeling that she was being watched.

She turned round slowly, but there was no one there. She had a good view all round her for some thirty feet before the walls of the ruined house rose here and there from the grassy ground, but she was definitely alone. Chiding herself for becoming as jumpy as a corn-fed thoroughbred, Sarah deliberately forced her nerves to calm themselves before putting on her straw hat. She tied the yellow ribbons under her chin, but as she pulled the bow tight she again had the feeling that she was being watched.

This time she couldn't make herself believe it was just nerves. The feeling was too strong to be denied. There was someone, she felt sure, somewhere behind one of the walls.

She began to feel alarmed.

She had wanted to explore further after her lunch, but now she changed her mind. All her enjoyment in the day was ruined, and she decided to head for home.

Home!

But yes, in some way she did not fully understand, Watermead Grange had become her home.

She picked up the picnic basket. As she did so she caught sight of movement out of the corner of her eye.

'Who's there?' she called. Her voice, she was pleased to discover, held no trace of nervousness or fear.

A minute later a figure emerged from behind one of the ruined walls, and Sarah nearly laughed out loud.

'Mr Haversage!' she exclaimed.

'Miss Davenport,' he said, coming towards her with a smile.

'But I thought you were in Ramsgate, visiting your sister,' she said, with far more enthusiasm than she would usually have shown for the boys' tutor. She was so relieved to discover he was not a footpad that she could even bear the thought of walking back to the

Grange in his company!

'My sister was feeling rather tired—she is in a delicate condition, you understand—and so I decided to cut short my visit and return a day or two earlier than planned. She refused to rest whilst I was staying with her and I didn't want her to overtax her strength, so I told her I needed a few days to prepare the boys' lessons. After that, she was happy to let me go a little sooner than arranged.'

'But what brought you to the ruins?' Sarah asked, as Mr Haversage fell into step beside her.

'I had time on my hands, and I have never been here before. It seemed the perfect chance,' said Mr Haversage. 'I didn't startle you, I hope?'

'No,' Sarah lied. She did not want him to know how nervous she had been. 'But I thought you *had* been here before,' she said with a frown. 'Surely you told me you knew the ruins well—'

'No,' he answered her forcefully.

'Oh, but I'm sure—'

'No. You are mistaken.'

Sarah did not press the point, but she began to have a return of the nervousness she had felt when she had known that she was being watched. Because Mr Haversage had definitely told her, several weeks before, that he knew the ruins well. Still, it was only a coincidence that he had met her here—wasn't it? He couldn't have come back even sooner than he had admitted to, could he, and knowing it was her day off, followed her from the Grange?

No. Of course not. Why would he?

There was an uncomfortable silence. 'And what do you think of the ruins?' she asked at last, breaking the silence and with an effort keeping her tone light.

'They are pleasant enough, but they are not as fine as the ruins at Reculver. Have you seen Reculver Towers?' he asked her. 'They are splendid; right on the coast, with the sea just a stone's throw away.'

Sarah, with her mind only half on the conversation, murmured, 'No. I've never been to Reculver.'

'Then you must let me take you there sometime.'

He spoke pleasantly but Sarah felt the small hairs rise on the back of her neck. Some instinct told her that he was not to be trusted, and she began to be afraid. She was alone with Mr Haversage, and far from help.

She was brought out of her thoughts by Mr Haversage looking at her curiously and saying, 'Are you all right?'

'Mm? Oh yes, quite all right.'

'You don't look all right,' he said. There was something almost satisfied about his expression as he said it.

'It's just that the basket's rather heavy,' she said, making an excuse.

‘Then you must let me carry it for you.’ He made a move to take it out of her hand.

‘No.’ Sarah spoke more vehemently than she had intended. ‘No. I can manage.’

‘Sarah . . .’ said Mr Haversage.

There was something unpleasant about the way he said it.

‘I don’t think you should call me that.’

‘Why not?’ He moved round so that he was standing in front of her. ‘We’re not at the Grange now. There’s no need for either of us to pretend.’

‘I don’t know what you’re talking about,’ she retorted, moving round him.

But he caught her by the arm and pulled her towards him. ‘You can’t hide it from me, Sarah. There’s no need. We both know what you feel for me—what we feel for each other.’

‘I assure you you’re mistaken,’ said Sarah, trying to keep her voice even as she pulled herself free.

‘Why deny it?’ he asked, following her, just half a step behind. ‘It’s nothing to be ashamed of. We could have a lot of fun together, you and I.’

‘I don’t think I’d like your idea of fun.’ Sarah quickened her step.

‘Oh, but I assure you you would.’

‘Get away from me,’ said Sarah, dropping all pretence of any kind of normality. There was something very menacing about Mr Haversage and she wanted to get away from him as quickly as she could.

'What? Before we've enjoyed each other?' he asked her, quickening his own step to match her own. 'Don't be a bloody little fool.'

He caught hold of her by the arm again and Sarah, seriously frightened now, swung out with the basket. It caught him a blow on the side. It was enough to make him loosen his hold. Then, seizing her opportunity, she picked up her skirts and ran. But he was hot on her heels and he caught her again, swinging her round, and she was horrified at the change in his face. It was twisted and brutal. With a rising feeling of panic she struggled to get away from him, but he held her more tightly, and in desperation she lifted her foot and brought it cracking down on his own. It was enough to make him let go of her and she wrenched herself free. As she did so he caught at her arm but succeeded only in catching hold of her sleeve. She pulled away from him. The delicate muslin ripped, but it was a small price to pay for her freedom and, with the shoulder of her dress torn, Sarah made the most of her lead to get away.

She was a good runner, and had often indulged in races with her brothers out on the moors near her Derbyshire home, but she knew that she could not outrun Mr Haversage for ever. Although his foot was giving him some pain, in the end he would catch her again. The road was her one hope of escape.

It was much quieter than the road from the Grange to the village, but still it was frequented, and as she fled from Mr Haversage she prayed that there would be some passing chaise or carriage. Because if not, her immediate future looked grim . . .

* * *

The week in London had not gone as well as Lord Randall had hoped. Although he had learnt that the Radicals were being controlled by a person of influence, probably someone who knew Kent well, which had set his mind working in new directions, he still had not been able to forget about Sarah.

It was true that, once back in London amongst the familiar landmarks, and amongst those of his friends who had not left town for the summer, he had felt anew all the impossibilities of becoming attached to a governess. But his feelings for Sarah had remained unchanged. In fact, it was only when he had left the Grange that he had begun to understand what an important part she played in his life. He had begun to learn things with Sarah that he had never known were possible. He had learnt that his nephews and niece responded to care and affection far more readily than they responded to endless discipline; he had learnt that he could not pigeon-hole people, and that not all governesses were humble and eager to please, and that it was a good thing they were not—he had learnt that it was not necessarily a bad thing if someone stood up to him; he had learnt that it was possible for him to have tender feelings, and to have them for a governess; and he had learnt that life was far more complicated than he had ever thought it could be.

So that now, as he returned to Watermead Grange, he was no nearer to solving the dilemma of his *most unusual* governess than he had been when he had left for London the week before.

Until he arrived back at the Grange he decided not to think any more about it. The day was fine and he was enjoying the journey. And so were the horses. The fierce heat of the earlier part of the summer had gone, to be replaced by cooler weather: perfect for tooling along the country roads that led to the Grange in the light and well-made curricle.

The horses, a well-matched pair of bays, sensed that they were nearing home and Lord Randall gave them their heads. Up ahead, just around a bend in the road, was the familiar ruined house that lay to the north of the estate, and once past there it would not be long before he turned into the impressive driveway that led to the Grange.

But as he negotiated the bend, slowing the horses with practised hands, all thought of the

Grange was pushed out of his mind by the sight of a familiar figure running from the ruins and making for the road just ahead of him.

He saw her only from the back, but there was no mistaking who she was.

'Sarah!' he cried, bringing the horses to a halt and leaving them snorting and stamping as he jumped down from the curricle, looping the reins over a nearby boulder.

She turned to face him and his blood turned to ice. He had never seen her looking so distraught. Her hair was coming loose from its pins and her yellow muslin was ripped across the shoulder.

'What happened?' he demanded, striding towards her and catching hold of her shoulders as he reached her.

She was so out of breath from running that she could not answer him, but she glanced over her shoulder, back towards the ruins, and he realized at once that someone was pursuing her.

A moment later Mr Haversage appeared, looking as Lord Randall had never seen him before. His face was contorted by a look of brutish violence, as though the civilized mask had been torn from his face to leave nothing but an animal behind.

'Haversage!' said Lord Randall grimly.

Mr Haversage slowed his step, hopping awkwardly once or twice before coming to a stop just inches away from Sarah.

With one firm movement James pulled her behind him, so that she was protected by his powerful frame.

'What the devil is the meaning of this?' he demanded, his eyes starting to smoulder.

Mr Haversage gave Lord Randall a sly look before shrugging. 'Miss Davenport and I were just . . . having a little fun,' he said.

'Insolent cur!' James took a step forward as he felt Sarah stiffen behind him. He was seized with a passionate desire to wipe the twisted smile from Haversage's face with his fist, and it was only with the greatest difficulty that he remembered his position and managed to stop himself in time. No matter what the provocation he was not going to lower himself by brawling with a common tutor, a man who was not even a gentleman. 'You will see me as soon as you return to the Grange,' he said instead, in his most arrogant manner, before turning and helping Sarah into the curricle.

Her hand as he held it was trembling, and he was filled with a longing to still her trembling with caresses and soothing words.

'I don't think I'll be returning to the Grange,' said Mr Haversage defiantly; he had recovered much of his suave manner. 'The post, I find, does not suit me.'

Lord Randall turned to him with a grim face.

'You are guilty of assault, Haversage, and

you will face me either in my capacity as your employer, or in my capacity as the local magistrate. The choice is yours.'

At this Mr Haversage's face darkened, but his insolence crumbled before Lord Randall's arrogance. 'Very well,' he muttered.

'This was an evil day's work, Haversage,' said Lord Randall as he climbed into his curricle with one powerful thrust of his legs and took up the reins. 'It is one you will regret.'

And so will you, my lord,' muttered Mr Haversage under his breath as the curricle pulled away from him. 'So will you.'

* * *

As she rode along in the curricle beside Lord Randall, Sarah felt completely drained. Her emotions had been through a series of rapid changes, from fear and panic when Mr Haversage had attacked her, to warmth and relief when James had taken charge of the situation and dealt with it in his uniquely arrogant way.

Arrogance and high-handedness! She had spent much of her time at the Grange railing against them but she was forced to admit that they had their uses after all!

But now, she wondered, what must Lord Randall think of her?

She tried to tell herself that it did not matter

what he thought, but she was disturbed to find that it *did* matter. It mattered very much. She wanted to explain to him, to make him understand.

She began hesitantly. 'I want you to know that I wasn't a party to—'

'Of course you weren't,' he snapped angrily, his anger, however, clearly directed at Mr Haversage and not at Sarah. 'How the dog had the audacity to suggest it I don't know.' He turned to look at her. 'Sarah,' he said more gently, 'I know you'd never be involved with someone like Haversage, and I know you would never go along with something like that. I'm only sorry that you had such a terrible experience. I hope Haversage hasn't put you off—' He stopped short, as if suddenly realizing what he was saying. *I hope Haversage hasn't put you off the thought of intimacy* he had been going to say, but to say any such thing to the children's governess would be going beyond all bounds of decency. So he corrected himself, and said, 'I hope Haversage hasn't put you off visiting the local beauty spots.'

'No,' said Sarah, as they turned into the drive. 'No, of course not. But I think the next time I have a day off I may not go out alone, all the same.'

'I will dismiss Haversage, of course.' He broke off with a frown, for the first time questioning his high-handed nature. 'That is, if you wish it.' The words came out with difficulty, but still they came out, and Sarah knew what they must have cost him. For Lord Randall to resist taking other people's decisions for them was a change in him indeed. She knew how used he was to taking decisions concerning everyone around him, and she knew how used he was to never having them questioned. But here he was, questioning himself. She had been right when she thought he had changed. Although he would always have an arrogant streak in his nature—and arrogance had its uses, she was forced to admit—he respected her enough to realize that she was capable of taking her own decisions, and that she had a right to do so. But in this case, her decision matched his own.

'Yes, I do wish it.' She hesitated. 'I don't think he's simply someone who took advantage of the situation. I think he may be unbalanced.'

He nodded. 'I think you may be right. I'll dismiss him as soon as he returns.' He thought for a moment. 'He may make difficulties. It's possible he may tell lies about what happened this afternoon, and blacken your character.'

'I'm not afraid of him,' said Sarah. 'Not any more. As soon as I saw you I knew I was safe.'

She would not have made such an admission if it had not been for the fact that she was still very shaken. But her words, direct and open, went straight to his heart. He had been longing to comfort her ever since he had seen her running out into the road, and he found that he could fight his feelings no more.

'Oh, to hell with this!' he said roughly, and passing the reins into his left hand he drew her towards him with his right, putting his arm around her and cradling her trembling form against his own firm body.

Sarah gave a deep sigh and relaxed against him. The last traces of the fear that had gripped her at the ruins dissolved. But the trembling did not stop. Because now it was caused by something other than fear . . .

She turned up her face to his.

He looked down into her eyes, longing to kiss her and, in a moment of madness, giving way to that longing. He retained just enough control to make sure he brushed only her cheek with his kiss, reminding himself over and over again that she was a governess and he was her employer, and that it would be unforgivable of him to take advantage of her—especially as he was all but engaged; and it was only this that stopped him from giving way to his feelings altogether and kissing her beautiful lips.

Sarah, feeling that she had emerged from a nightmare to find herself in a dream, nestled closer to him.

It could not last, this moment. It was out of time; unreal; prompted by Mr Haversage's unpardonable behaviour. But for one moment she allowed herself to imagine what it would be like if she and James had been equals, and the thought made her heart turn over.

But they were not equals, she reminded herself with a sinking of her spirits as the Grange came into sight. They were earl and governess. And Lord Randall would never forget it.

Slowly he released her, and she was conscious of an emptiness she had not known before. Reluctantly she pulled away from him, putting her dreams aside.

With light hands he slowed the horses until the curricle had come to a stop.

The eyes he turned on her were unreadable. 'If we return to the stables together, with your dress torn . . .'

'. . . it will give rise to gossip. I'll walk back to the Grange from here.'

'You don't have to . . .'

'I want to. Mr Haversage may spread rumours about what happened this afternoon but that doesn't mean I have to fuel them. I'm not likely to see anyone at this hour. Once I'm back in my room I can soon change my dress, and then no one will be any the wiser.'

He nodded, and as he helped her down from the curricle his admiration for her courage was plain to see.

Sarah recovered the picnic basket from the curricle and then, lifting her chin, she made her way back to the Grange.

CHAPTER NINE

Mr Haversage was sullen. He stood in front of Lord Randall in the latter's study like a naughty schoolboy. His hands were thrust into the pockets of his breeches and his face wore a scowl.

'Have you anything to say for yourself?' asked Lord Randall.

Mr Haversage gave an insolent shrug. 'Only that what I do in my free time is up to me—and what Miss Davenport does in her free time is up to her,' he added with a suggestive leer.

Lord Randall did not rise to the bait. He knew perfectly well that Sarah had not been a willing party to Mr Haversage's advances, and knew that the tutor was simply trying to get under his skin.

'It will go better for you if you don't try to blacken Miss Davenport's name,' he said evenly.

'What's the matter, Randall?' asked Mr Haversage. 'Can't you face the thought of the governess preferring me to you? It hurts your pride, does it, that she'd rather dally with a tutor than an earl?'

Lord Randall looked at Mr Haversage as though he was a vile insect but made no reply to the insolent question, and continued as though it had never been spoken. 'As you have nothing to say, no apology to make, then I have no choice but to dismiss you.'

Mr Haversage made a noise of disgust. 'What a hypocrite. Dismissing me for doing something you want to do yourself.' He gave an unpleasant smile. 'I've seen the way you look at her. You wouldn't mind her clothes being ripped off if it was you doing the ripping, would you?' he said with a sneer.

Lord Randall had been afraid that, if the interview turned ugly, he would be tempted to lay Mr Haversage out, but his earlier rage was now firmly under control. Everything Mr Haversage said, instead of making his blood run hotter, made it colder and colder. So that now his voice was icy as he said, 'Thank you, Haversage. I couldn't decide whether or not to give you a reference—your work with the boys has been adequate after all—but you have made my decision for me. You will leave Watermead Grange at once. What you do in the future is up to you. But you will have no reference to help you find another post.'

'I wouldn't want one,' Mr Haversage sneered. 'I have better things to do with my life than teaching stuck-up little brats.'

Lord Randall stood up. He towered over Mr Haversage. 'I suggest you leave immediately,' he said, his brow darkening.

'I can't wait to go,' said Mr Haversage. He made for the door. But he could not resist turning round and making a parting shot. 'Good luck with her, Randall. Give her a—*kiss*—from me.'

The smirk that accompanied this remark left no doubt about what he really meant by the word *kiss*.

'Get out,' said Lord Randall.

'With pleasure.' Mr Haversage almost spat the words. And then, turning, he left the room, banging the door behind him.

* * *

Although Sarah was of a naturally buoyant nature she had been upset by the incident with Mr Haversage, not least because of the way it had affected her feelings for James. No matter how many times she told herself that their closeness had been unreal, no matter how many times she told herself it had been a moment out of time, she could not forget the heat of his body or the strength of his embrace.

She was making the most of the morning by gathering a collection of flowers in the small woodland to the side of the house. She had promised Lucy she would teach her how to press wild flowers and knew that it would be easier for her to gather them now, before the guests for the house-party started to arrive. Once the party began in earnest there would be guests everywhere, and it would be better for her to stay in the schoolroom.

Having collected an armful of suitable specimens she made her way back to the house.

'Miss Davenport,' said Hodgess, materializing out of nowhere. 'His lordship is looking for you, miss. He would like you to join him in the ballroom.'

Sarah felt a moment of surprise and then, saying, 'Thank you, Hodgess,' turned her steps in that direction. She felt her heart beating faster as she walked. It was the first time she had seen Lord Randall since their intimate journey in his curricle. How should she react?

Why, the same as always came her next thought as her good sense came to her aid. It had been a temporary lapse, nothing more, and it would be best if she behaved as though nothing untoward had ever happened.

She went into the ballroom. Lord Randall was standing at the far end, with the estate carpenters. Sarah felt relieved. It would be much easier to meet him in company, rather than alone. In company there would be no opportunity for the encounter to get out of hand, as all their recent encounters had seemed to do.

'Lord Randall? Hodgess said you wished to see me?'

He turned round. His black eyes lit at the sight of her. 'Beautiful,' he said.

Her heart fluttered.

‘The flowers,’ he said, after a lengthy pause.

‘Oh, yes. Yes, of course,’ she said, recovering herself. ‘I’m going to teach Lucy how to press them.’

‘A good idea. She’ll enjoy that, I’m sure.’

One of the carpenters cleared his throat.

‘It’s partly because of Lucy I asked you to join me. I’m thinking of having a temporary dais built at the end of the ballroom. I thought the children might enjoy having a stage to perform on, as they are so small that they might not be seen otherwise. What do you think of the idea?’

‘I think it’s a good one,’ said Sarah, as she imagined it in her mind’s eye. The room was a long one, with french windows giving out on to the terrace at the right. A dais at the end would raise the children nicely. ‘Yes,’ she nodded.

‘They won’t find it intimidating?’

‘No, I don’t think so. They’ve become much more confident recently. I think they’ll find it exciting.’

‘And you?’

Sarah imagined herself sitting on the dais, playing the pianoforte to accompany Lucy’s singing. ‘I think I might enjoy it, too.’ She smiled, pleased that he had thought of her feelings. In manner he may have returned to what he had been before she was assaulted by Mr Haversage, but his protective instinct remained.

'Good.' He turned to the carpenters. 'I want it ready as soon as possible.'

Sarah took the opportunity of excusing herself and slipping out of the door. Although she had found their meeting easier than expected under the circumstances, memories of him drawing her towards him and dropping kisses on her head kept intruding, and she felt it was better to be elsewhere. Now that this first meeting was over she knew she would find it easier to talk to him next time they met. But for now, she felt it was better not to overtax her self-control.

She went up to the schoolroom, where Lucy, who had been getting dressed, now joined her, and the two of them began sorting the flowers. It was an enjoyable occupation and, together with pressing them and writing notes about them, took most of the day.

Lucy had just finished pressing the last one when there was a crunching sound on the gravel below. A carriage! The first of Lord Randall's guests had arrived.

'All right,' said Sarah kindly, answering Lucy's hopeful gaze, 'you can go and have a look.'

Lucy flashed her a smile and then skipped over to the window, where she stood on tiptoe so that she could see out. Sarah followed her to keep an eye on her, and because she was just as interested as Lucy was in Lord Randall's guests.

From the attic window the carriage looked like a toy, and the lady who stepped out of it looked like a tiny doll, but even so, Sarah could see that her clothes were magnificent.

'What a wonderful hat,' she sighed, as she watched the ostrich-plumes bobbing up and down in the breeze. For a moment she was lost in her memories, thinking of the days when she, too, had gone to parties. Oh! None so grand as the party that was beginning at the Grange, but enjoyable parties for all that.

She ran her hands unconsciously over the rough, cheap muslin of the gown she was wearing now. How harsh it felt! How different from the gowns she had been used to; for although her family had not had much money, her father had always made sure she had a pretty dress or two for local balls. And how different from her rough muslin was the wonderful cambric carriage-dress of the lady who descended from the next equipage. Even from this distance Sarah could see that it was elaborately trimmed with frills, and that the lady's parasol was trimmed to match.

'That's Mrs de Bracy,' said Lucy knowledgeably.

'How do you know that?' asked Sarah curiously.

'She often comes here,' confided Lucy. 'Hanson'—Hanson was Lucy's nurse—'Hanson says she's no better than she ought to be. Then she sniffs.' Here Lucy gave a little sniff of her own, in imitation of Hanson. It was a wonderful copy, full of disdain! 'And then she says,' Lucy went on, ' "But Lord Randall is a *man*, after all, and a man has *needs*".'

Sarah would have smiled at Lucy's clever impersonation of her nurse, particularly the way her voice had darkened towards the end, if the words had not come as such a shock. Lucy, of course, had no idea what Hanson meant, but Sarah knew. In all the time she had been at Watermead Grange she had never thought about Lord Randall's life away from the Grange, and it was like cold water thrown over her face to realize that Mrs de Bracy was in all probability his mistress.

She turned away from the window.

She felt hot and sick inside. Her stomach was churning. She tried to overcome the feeling by focusing her attention on the books on her desk but she could not concentrate. She had never felt like that in her life before, but she was powerless to do anything about it.

She did not want to acknowledge the emotion, but she had no choice. It was jealousy.

Lucy was too interested in the scene unfolding before her to notice that Sarah had left her side. Another lady and two gentlemen followed the first lady out of the carriage, and then all four of them disappeared into the front door of the Grange.

Lucy watched the carriage with interest as

the horseman whipped up the horses and the carriage rolled away, crunching on the gravel as it made its way round to the coach house. And no sooner had it disappeared than another took its place.

She continued to watch the guests arrive, until Sarah, mastering her emotion, called the little girl away. 'You have seen enough for now, Lucy. Let us get back to work.'

* * *

Laughter filled the house. Gaiety and music and light abounded, as Lord Randall entertained his guests. But behind his smile he was ill at ease. As the party had progressed he had become more and more irritated by Miss Leatherhead, and the worst of it was, it was not her fault. She had not changed. She was still what she had been in London: meek, respectful, quiet and biddable—everything he had thought he could want from a wife. She came from an old and distinguished family; she was extremely pretty; and she would defer to him on all things at all times.

But wasn't that the fault?

She would never stand up to him, not even when he was wrong.

As he watched her talking to young Lord Brancaster at dinner one night, her golden curls gleaming in the candlelight, and her blue eyes turned trustingly up to the young lord's, he realized Miss Leatherhead would be incapable of standing up to a mouse!

Why did he find that unsatisfactory? he wondered. Why did he think that a wife with the courage to stand up to him was what he wanted instead? Why did he think that marrying a young lady who would leave him untouched and unchanged would be a waste? Why did he want the challenge of animated company? Of the cut and thrust of conversation? The exchange of ideas?

The answer to that was all too obvious.

But he dare not acknowledge it. Even to himself.

* * *

The time passed in a whirl of enjoyable activities for Lord Randall's guests: archery, riding and boating by day; eating, dancing and music by night. But for Lord Randall himself the time passed rather differently. Not only did he realize with each passing day how impossible it would be for him to marry Miss Leatherhead, but he was also unsettled by the fact that he had not got any further with the Radical affair. He watched and listened, dropping discreet questions into the conversation and trying to find out which, if any, of his guests could be Radicals, but so far he was not having any luck.

'What a wonderful ball, Lord Randall,'

called Mrs Leatherhead on the final evening, as she glided across the ballroom towards him like a galleon in full sail. She came to a stop in front of him and unfurled her enormous fan.

'Margaret thinks it is a wonderful ball, too,' she declared.

'Oh, yes,' murmured Miss Leatherhead prettily. She had been towed along in her mama's wake, and smiled sweetly up at Lord Randall.

Lord Randall made her a polite bow, but his thoughts were troubled. He felt it would be wrong of him to propose to Miss Leatherhead, now that his feelings had undergone a change, but this left him in an awkward position. He had paid her a great deal of attention whilst in London for the Season and could not now draw back without damaging her reputation.

'We are so looking forward to the children's concert, Lord Randall,' said Mrs Leatherhead mendaciously, fortunately knowing nothing of his thoughts. 'Margaret has been looking forward to it all day.'

'Oh, yes,' said Margaret dutifully.

'Such a . . . such an *interesting* idea. So . . . unusual.'

James smiled. 'Indeed it is. "Unusual" is the very word for it. But then, it was arranged by a very unusual person.'

'Oh indeed, indeed,' agreed Mrs Leatherhead and James was amused to discover that she thought he had been referring to himself. 'Unusual in every way. Quite unique!'

'Oh, yes,' said Margaret, and then added another word—greatly daring!—'indeed.'

'Then if we are all looking forward to it, I suggest we take our places.'

He guided the ladies to the front of the ballroom, which was elegantly proportioned and had french windows down one side, leading on to the terrace. He helped them to take their places before the dais that had been erected at the far end. Rows of chairs had been arranged in front of it, and as James took his place in the middle of the front row his other guests began to follow suit.

The chairs surrounding James filled up quickly as the ladies, particularly the unmarried ones, struggled to sit as close to him as possible. It was an annoyance. But as a wealthy widower he knew there was nothing he could do to avoid such attentions and bore it with good grace.

'Such a lovely party, Lord Randall,' gushed Miss Annabelle Cartwright, who had rushed to get the seat behind him.

'And such a wonderful concert,' added her mother, blithely ignoring the fact that it had not even begun. 'What a good idea to have the children to entertain us. Little angels! Annabelle is so fond of children. What a mother she will make.'

'Oh, Mama! You'll put me to the blush!'

giggled Annabelle.

James gave a wry smile. Both mother and daughter took it as a hopeful sign—they neither of them gave up on any gentleman until he was well and truly married, and were not in the least disturbed by the rumours that he was about to propose to Miss Leatherhead—but they would have been disappointed to know that Lord Randall, instead of picturing Annabelle as the mother of his children, was remembering the way in which she had snapped repeatedly at her brother on a picnic the previous year. He therefore judged her 'love of children' accordingly!

By seven o'clock, the time appointed for the small concert to begin, every chair was full, and if some of the gentlemen were more interested in the drinks they held in their hands, and if some of the ladies were more interested in the gentlemen, well, that was only to be expected.

But James found that he was genuinely interested to see what the children had learnt. He had agreed to the concert because he had realized that what Sarah had said was true: the children *did* need to be able to win his approval. And although this was not the way he would have chosen, he trusted Sarah's judgement enough to go along with the idea.

As the clock in the hall struck the hour the door opened and the children filed in. Lucy was looking exquisite in a silken dress and pantaloons, her hair falling in ringlets over her shoulder and decorated with an adorable pink ribbon. In fact, she looked very much as she had looked at Lady Templeton's home, now almost three months ago. But with this difference. That, whereas before, she had been crammed into pretty but restrictive clothes all the time, whether she wanted to be or not, now she had chosen her outfit, and was enjoying 'being dressed up'. Fitzwilliam and Preston, too, were looking very smart, and there was a general murmur of approval when the three children took their places on the small stage.

Sarah followed them and sat at the pianoforte, ready to accompany Lucy's singing.

There were a few interested glances from the males in the audience, and a few patronizing looks from the ladies, who ran their eyes loftily over Sarah's simple muslin dress. But, seeing the shabby state of it, they were prepared to concede that Miss Davenport seemed 'a good kind of girl'.

There were the usual coughs and fidgeting whilst the audience settled themselves. Then, arranging their features into suitably interested expressions, they waited for the concert to begin.

Lucy was the first to perform. She walked over to the pianoforte, amongst coos of delight from the ladies, and stood beside Sarah. She folded her hands in front of her and turned out her toes. Sarah played the introduction and Lucy began to sing. Her voice was sweet, and Sarah was delighted with her efforts, particularly when the song was greeted with a round of applause—a round of applause which was heartily led by James.

Fitzwilliam and Preston performed equally well, if not better, and Sarah was left with a feeling of intense satisfaction that she had managed to persuade James to allow the concert, and that the children had done so well.

As the applause began to die away, Sarah led the children out of the room. It had been a wonderful experience for them, but now it was time for them to leave the adults, and for Lucy to go to bed.

Things began to return to normal. After a few exclamations of, 'Oh! How charming!' and 'Good lord! Sparky little whippersnappers!' the guests began to leave their seats and think about the supper to come.

Lord Randall, however, could only think about the children and how well they had done. And about their governess. Despite the simplicity of her dress, he had found her more beautiful than any other woman there. Hers was a beauty lit from within, by the strength and humour of her character. And what strength she had had: to perform in front of so many people and yet, instead of giving way to nerves herself, she had given courage and confidence to the children. She really was truly remarkable.

As they left the room, he followed, and caught up with them before they reached the stairs.

'Well done, children,' he said. He was now relaxed with the children, and he was soon deep in conversation with the boys, asking them about their pieces and praising them for their efforts.

Sarah was delighted to see Lord Randall's obvious interest, and glowed when she realized how well they were all getting on together.

And then Lucy. Lord Randall turned his attention to the little girl and Lucy, suddenly shy, stood on one leg, clutching the other behind her. It was something Sarah had not seen her do since their first meeting at Lady Templeton's house, and she realized how Lucy must feel. Lord Randall was looking particularly magnificent this evening, in a black tail-coat, cream pantaloons, frilled shirt and a silk cravat. A diamond tie-pin added to his air of magnificence, and it was not surprising Lucy was overawed.

But Lord Randall soon put her at her ease. Kneeling down beside her he said affectionately, 'I enjoyed your singing, Lucy.'

A slow smile spread over her face and she murmured, 'Thank you, Uncle James!'

The smile on Lucy's face brought an answering smile to his own and before long the two of them were chatting away merrily.

'Well done, children,' said Sarah, as Lord Randall stood up. 'Now: time for bed.'

There were a few moans, but not too many. The day had been exciting, and even Fitzwilliam and Preston felt that they would not mind having an early night.

'I expect you to return to the ballroom when you have handed the children over to their nurse,' Lord Randall said. Being with Sarah had been as refreshing as a cool drink on a hot and muggy day and he realized that he no longer wanted to talk to the insipid people who were floating round his house. He wanted to talk to Sarah. He missed the honesty and openness of her company.

Sarah had no suitable clothes to wear, but she had a sudden longing to enjoy the sights and sounds of a ballroom again. Even though she knew she would be nothing but a wallflower she could not resist the temptation to agree. Particularly as she knew that James—Lord Randall, she corrected herself—would not let her refuse.

She gave him an impish smile. 'Of course, my lord,' she replied mischievously as she picked up her skirts and led the children upstairs. 'Just whatever you say!'

CHAPTER TEN

Supper was over by the time Sarah returned to the ballroom. Lord Randall's guests, all by now very well fed, milled about with less energy than before. But still the scene looked dazzling to Sarah, who had seen nothing like it for years. Crystal chandeliers hung from the ceilings. The light from the hundreds of candles, reflected in the mirrors that lined the wall opposite the open french doors, lit up the scene with a brightness that was close to day. Elegant ladies in silks and satins paraded round the room, wafting themselves with their charming lace fans. The gentlemen congregated in corners, or drifted into an adjoining room to play cards. A small orchestra played, and one or two couples had enough energy left to dance.

Sarah made her way through the room, drinking in the sights and sounds that had once been so familiar to her. Eyebrows were raised as she walked past. One or two ladies pulled their trains out of the way, as though not wanting to be contaminated by mixing with a governess. But Sarah was so engrossed that she did not notice.

Having walked through the ballroom she realized there was no one she knew there. She had expected to find James there, as well as

Dominic and the other people she had met at the boating-party, but she realized they must all be outside or in the card-room.

She was just deciding what she should do next when strains of conversation drifted in through the open french doors. She was about to move away so that she would not overhear someone else's conversation when the word 'Derbyshire' caught her ear.

'Do you know Derbyshire at all?' a man's voice was saying.

A chorus of 'No', 'Can't say I do, Farbey', and '*Is* there such a place?'—this last from Mr Horsham, who accounted himself a great wit!—followed the question, and without more ado the first voice proceeded to recount the many delights of that county.

Sarah's face grew puzzled, as she could not but help overhearing what was being said.

'Is something wrong?' asked James when he joined her a few minutes later, seeing the puzzled expression on her face.

'No, nothing,' she said with a smile, pleased that he had found her.

He looked at her intently. *Something* must have caused her puzzled face.

'It's just that . . .' she began. Then she gave a small shrug. 'Oh, it was nothing. Just something I overheard, that's all. It struck me as . . . odd.'

'A mystery,' he said, smiling. He guided her out on to the terrace, away from the disapproving stares of the unmarried young ladies and their matchmaking mamas, who did not take kindly to Lord Randall paying attention to his governess—absurd idea!—when he should be paying attention to them instead. 'There's nothing better than a good mystery to liven up a dull party.'

'It seems very bright to me,' remarked Sarah.

'It is now,' he remarked meaningfully, with a warm light in his eyes. Then he went on, 'What is it that startled you? If there's a mystery, two heads are better than one.'

Sarah gave a slight shiver, the night being cool, and James had to resist the temptation to draw her close. 'Do you want to go in?' he asked.

'No.' Her reply was definite.

He nodded. 'Miss Davenport's shawl,' he called to a passing footman.

'Yes, my lord. At once, my lord.'

'I'm all right,' said Sarah, pleased none the less with his considerateness.

But the footman, to whom Lord Randall's word was law, had already gone to fetch it.

'So what is your mystery, Sarah?' he asked as they strolled along the terrace.

She shook her head. 'Hardly a mystery. It's just that I overheard someone, a man called Farbey, though whether he's Mr or Sir or Lord—'

'Lord,' interrupted James.

'—talking about Derbyshire.'

'Ah!' James smiled. 'Yes. I'd forgotten Farbey had chosen Derbyshire for his retreat. Farbey is a local landowner,' he explained to Sarah. 'He lost a lot of money at the gaming-tables recently and had to live quietly for a while, allowing him to rent out his estate and restore at least a part of his fortune. You have met his tenants; they are the Wilberforces. Farbey has returned to Kent to renew the lease, but will be going back to Derbyshire next week.'

'But the things he said . . .' Sarah's voice was puzzled. 'They didn't make sense.' She stopped walking. James stopped beside her. 'I know the area well, but it seemed—well, ridiculous as it sounds, it seemed as though he had never been there. He described Upper Cross as a village, and Upper Cross is a town. A sizeable town.' Her brow was furrowed.

'People have different ideas of villages and towns,' said James. 'Farbey has spent a lot of his life in London, and provincial towns most probably seem like villages to him.'

'But it wasn't only the places,' Sarah continued, unconvinced by the reason he had suggested. 'It was the people as well. He said that he often visited the Drumptons at Buxton; in fact, he said they were the most important family in the neighbourhood.'

'Well, what of it?'

'There are no Drumptons in Buxton.'

James's voice took on an edge. There was an alertness in his tone that had not been there before.

'Are you sure about this?'

'Of course I am.'

'It couldn't be,' said James, more to himself than Sarah. 'He couldn't have stayed here to organize the Radical group I'm looking for. Could he? Simply saying that he'd gone to Derbyshire as a blind? No. He's rented out the house. He couldn't have stayed here without its being generally known.'

'Ah!' Sarah, following her own train of thought, gave a satisfied sigh, as though she had just solved a problem that had been worrying her. 'So that's where I've heard the name Farbey before. I knew it was familiar. It was Sam, the gardener's boy, who mentioned it when he was telling me about old Reverend Merriweather. He said that old Reverend Merriweather lives in one of Farbey's cottages down by the sea.' She broke off as she noticed James's face. 'Is there something wrong?'

He spoke slowly. 'I think there might be.' He had forgotten that Farbey owned a number of remote cottages; Farbey could easily have stayed in one of them undetected if he had wanted to. He put his hands on Sarah's arms and looked down into her eyes. She felt a tingling sensation run up her arms and down her spine . . .

'Sarah, I have to leave you . . .'

'I've already stayed downstairs too long. I have to prepare . . .'

'No. That isn't what I meant. I want you to wait for me. Will you meet me on the terrace in ten minutes' time?'

Sarah nodded.

He hesitated, as if wondering how much to say.

'I won't be gone long, but it's very important you don't mention this to anyone else. Particularly not to Farbey.'

'It's significant, isn't it?' she asked, trying to gauge what the matter could be by looking into his face.

'It is. I can't tell you what it is yet—there is someone I have to talk to first.'

Sarah nodded, and James reluctantly took his hands from her arms. He turned and went back into the ballroom, finally disappearing through one of the doors that led into the hall.

Sarah, too, returned to the ballroom but she was not alone for long. First, the footman brought her her shawl. Then Mr Masterson, who had seen her go out on to the terrace with Lord Randall earlier, and had been waiting for his opportunity to speak to her, lost no time in joining her.

'I was hoping I would see you here tonight,' he said, having detached himself from the small group of people he had been talking to.

'Mr Masterson,' Sarah acknowledged him.

'You are looking very charming, if I may say

so.'

Sarah gave him a quizzical look.

He smiled. 'It takes more than fashionable clothes to make someone look charming,' he told her. 'And more than unfashionable ones to extinguish true beauty.'

Sarah smiled. 'You're flattering me.'

He smiled. 'Perhaps. But it is true, none the less.' He paused, then continued on a new note. 'Tell me, Miss Davenport, do you play cards?'

'I do,' she said, wondering where the conversation was leading.

'Then might I trouble you for a hand?'

'Willingly,' Sarah agreed. Mr Masterson was a pleasant and courteous gentleman, and she had no objection to playing a hand of piquet with him until James returned.

'I thought the children performed very well tonight,' he said as he guided her into the card-room. 'You have done a great deal for them, Miss Davenport. The concert was surprisingly enjoyable.'

'They worked very hard,' Sarah pointed out.

'And you, too, must have worked hard.'

Sarah noticed with surprise that the card-room was empty, except for a very deaf old dowager nursing a grumpy lap-dog.

Mr Masterson was less surprised. He had already noticed that it was almost empty, and he had invited Sarah to play a hand of cards with him because of this fact. The dowager's presence was enough to prevent the situation from being improper, but it suited him to have an almost empty room so that he could say what he wanted to say.

'Miss Davenport.' He hesitated. They had just reached one of the card-tables, and he wanted to prevent Sarah from sitting down. He felt sure that he would find it easier to say what he had to say if they were not separated by a table.

To her surprise, instead of sitting at the table, he turned to her with a look of great earnestness and said, 'Miss Davenport. Before we begin—that is to say—there is something I want to say to you. I think you must have some idea of what it is.'

Sarah looked at him blankly; so blankly that he realized she had no idea of what was in his mind.

That made it more difficult. But still, it was something he was determined to do.

'Miss Davenport, we have only known each other a short while, but already I feel that we are friends. When I met you at the boating-party I realized you were someone I could respect, someone I could work with—in short, what I am trying to say is that, although not wealthy, I am happily a prosperous man. I have a comfortable home, a comfortable income, and have, I believe, no real vices. I could perhaps not offer a wife an exciting life, but I could offer her a respectable and enjoyable one.'

'I'm sure you could,' she replied politely.

Mr Masterson, uncomfortably aware that she had not realized his speech had a point to it, took her hands in his. She was so surprised that she left them there. It felt pleasant. It felt very much as it had felt when her brothers had taken her hands before her family had been separated. Nice, cool and pleasant.

So that it did not prepare for his next words.

'Sarah—I hope I may soon have a right to call you by that name—Sarah, I would like you to be my wife.'

Sarah's eyes widened in surprise, and then she felt a rush of colour to her cheeks. How could she have been so stupid? If her mind had not been elsewhere she would have guessed what he was about and would have been able to stop him before he went too far. As it was, she was faced with the sad task of having to disappoint him.

'You do me too great an honour,' she said, withdrawing her hands from his.

'Don't say "no".'

'We hardly know each other,' she pointed out.

'We will come to know each other. Many people marry without knowing each other beforehand and go on to be very happy. My father and mother met only twice before they were married and they enjoyed forty years of happily married life.'

Sarah shook her head. 'I could not do that,' she said.

'I think it would be for your good, as well as for mine, if you said "yes". I believe I could make you happy.'

'If I could accept you, I would. But I can't,' she said gently.

'I have rushed you,' he said. 'Say nothing now, but give me leave to hope that—'

'No.' Sarah was firm. Mr Masterson was a good man, and she could not let a good man believe she might change her mind when she knew full well that she never would.

'Never the less, my offer remains open. If you should reconsider, a brief message will bring me to the Grange. You deserve more than the life of a governess, Sarah. I can give you that life. I can give you a respectable establishment; and in time, perhaps, there would be children of your own.'

The picture he painted was an attractive one, and Mr Masterson was an attractive man. Nevertheless, Sarah's answer remained unchanged.

'That is very generous of you, but I can never marry you, Mr Masterson. I don't love you and I could never marry where I do not love.'

He inclined his head. 'I see. Then I will trouble you no more.' He paused awkwardly. It would be unchivalrous of him to leave Sarah alone in the card-room, but he no longer felt equal to a game of piquet.

Understanding his dilemma, Sarah saved him from it by saying, 'If you will excuse me, Mr Masterson, I find I am not equal to a game of cards. Perhaps I could find you another partner for your game?'

But, as she had expected, he took the opportunity to excuse himself she had offered him, and withdrew.

Sarah took a turn around the room after he had gone, reflecting on the opportunity he had offered her. He was a good man, but she never once regretted her decision. It was true that, for some people, love blossomed after marriage, but Sarah knew that it would not have done so for her. She felt nothing when she was near Mr Masterson, except perhaps a sense of friendship, and for Sarah that was not enough.

A hubbub of conversation broke out at the door. A party of guests had decided they were bored with the orchestra playing in the ballroom and had decided to have a few hands of cards instead.

A few unfriendly looks were directed at Sarah.

Recalled to her situation, she excused herself and left the card-room. Then she returned to the terrace where she had arranged to meet James.

*   *   *

'What do you think?' asked James.

He was in the library, standing by the fireplace. Sitting in a deeply-buttoned leather chair opposite him was General Abercrombie, James's former commanding officer and his contact in the Radical affair.

The general stroked his white moustaches.

'It's possible. Perhaps probable. Yes, Farbey could be the man we're looking for: someone who's organizing a group of Radicals to keep in touch with Napoleon's supporters, so that if the former Emperor escapes from Elba—we should never have imprisoned him on Elba, Randall, it's far too close for comfort—so that if the former Emperor escapes then the Radicals will have advance warning, giving them time to organize an uprising over here to take place as soon as the army leaves Britain to go and fight Napoleon again. Yes, Farbey fits the bill. He's an influential man, with good organizational abilities. A landowner, but a disillusioned one.'

'And his land is mortgaged to the hilt,' James put in.

The general nodded.

'Once wealthy, now bankrupt, he may well be dissatisfied with his lot.'

'Bankrupt through his own vices,' remarked James.

'But still bankrupt. He has nothing to lose by joining the Radicals, and perhaps everything to gain. Yes. Farbey bears watching.'

'Then I'll have him followed,' said James. 'It will be interesting to see if he really returns to Derbyshire. If not, it will be even more interesting to see where he does go.'

The general stroked his moustaches again. 'Better if your hand isn't seen in this, Randall. You're useful to us down here. Once we've picked up Farbey—if Farbey is the ringleader—there may be others, either now or in the future. We need you to be above suspicion.'

James nodded. Anyone could have Farbey followed and picked up, but James was uniquely placed to gather information. It would be a waste for him to become too deeply involved.

'We'll have him followed and let you know the result,' said the general. He took a drink of brandy from the glass next to his hand. 'What put you on to it?' he asked. 'What put you on to the Derbyshire thing?'

James gave a wry smile. 'Miss Davenport. She overheard him talking and, because she used to live in Derbyshire, she realized that what he said didn't make any sense.'

'The governess?' The general sounded surprised. 'Must be an unusual filly.'

James smiled. 'She is.'

'This could be just the break we need,' said the general. 'A good piece of work, Randall. Well done.'

The general left to set things in motion, and James headed towards the terrace, where he hoped Sarah would be waiting for him.

But instead of finding Sarah there, he found Maud de Bracy.

'Why, James,' she said, going towards him with a seductive smile. 'I haven't seen you all evening. I was beginning to think you had deserted me.'

Maud had not been best pleased with the party so far. True, she was beginning to doubt whether James would indeed propose to Miss Leatherhead, but instead she had discovered something far worse: James was attracted to Miss Davenport.

To lose James to Margaret Leatherhead would have been tolerable, but to lose him to a governess was unbearable. Contrary to Hanson's belief, Maud and James were not lovers, but not from any lack of trying on Maud's part. She had wanted James for years, and she realized that if she did not make a play for him now it would soon be too late.

'It was such a good idea to hold a house-party. I have had a most delicious week. Still'—she gave him an arch look—'it could be even better.' She moved closer to him. 'Boating and concerts are all very well, but there are other, more adult pleasures we could enjoy.'

As she spoke she moved so close to him that her body was touching his. She smiled seductively and put her hand up to stroke his face.

He caught her wrist. 'Try to remember that you are a lady,' he said coldly.

He was in no mood for Maud's flirting. In fact he never had been. He had never really liked her—he merely tolerated her for politeness's sake; and the disdain he felt for her showed in his eyes.

His expression was a direct challenge to her. She wanted to wipe it off his face and replace it with one of lust instead.

As he relaxed his grip she brought her wrist in to her chest and pushed his hand on to her breast, at the same time reaching up and kissing him on the mouth.

He pushed her away, contempt written all over his face; but catching sight of movement to his right he turned his head and was just in time to see Sarah's shocked face, and then to see her running down the terrace steps and into the darkened grounds beyond.

'Damn you, Maud!' he said forcefully, thrusting her from him and following Sarah down the steps, his long legs taking them three at a time. There was only one thought in his mind; to find Sarah and tell her that what she had seen was misleading.

He didn't care what anyone else thought. He didn't care if the whole of London thought he was having an affair with Maud. But he couldn't bear for Sarah to think it.

'Sarah!' he called. 'Sarah!'

There was no answer. He came to a stop, looking round through the starlit dark to see which way she had gone. He heard a rustle; he headed towards it; he saw her.

'Sarah!'

He ran after her. She quickened her step, but she could not escape him. He caught her arm as she ran into the woodland that bordered the lawns.

'Sarah!'

She swallowed as she turned towards him. Her face was as white as a ghost.

'Sarah.' His voice was tender.

'Lord Randall,' she said, struggling to control the wild and stormy emotions that were raging in her breast.

He dropped her arm. He was breathing hard.

'Sarah. What you saw. On the—'

But by now Sarah had recovered her dignity. 'Saw, Lord Randall? You must be mistaken. I saw nothing.'

He looked at her with such a mixture of longing and concern that she felt her emotions threatening to break through her composed façade.

'You must be distraught. I have never heard you utter a falsehood before.'

'I . . .' She checked. It was true. Her nature was open and honest. Honest to a fault.

'What you saw was misleading,' he said.

‘It is none of my concern,’ she said, turning away from him. She could not talk about it. It was too painful for her.

‘It is your concern, Sarah. Mrs de Bracy wants a lover, but I could never be attracted to a woman like that. I am attracted to—’

He stopped himself just in time.

Sarah, knowing that her emotions were about to break the barriers she had set around them, wrenched her eyes from his and turned away.

She knew now why she had rejected Mr Masterson; knew now why she had felt as though a knife was twisting inside her when she had seen James with Maud. It was because of her feelings for James.

But he had said nothing about his feelings for her.

She ran on through the woodland but in the dark she tripped over a root and fell.

His arms were around her before she knew what was happening, and then his mouth was on hers. The contact unleashed an explosion of sensation as the energy that had crackled between them since their first meeting ignited and she was lost to all else. Her whole body was in the kiss; her whole mind, her whole heart, her whole spirit; everything she was. She kissed him hungrily, awakened to a fierce joy she had never dreamed existed.

And he, lost in her as she was lost in him, had to fight his body with all his strength to stop him making love to her right there on the woodland floor.

She was unlike anyone he had ever known, and she had aroused feelings in him that went beyond anything he had ever experienced. This was different. This was not just the slaking of lust. This had meaning. This had new levels of awareness and sensation. This took him into unexplored territory.

He pulled back, wanting to look at her, taking her face between his hands and gazing down into her face.

'Sarah . . .'

But temptation was too strong, and his voice was lost as he showered her with passionate kisses, making her dizzy and weak.

At last he let her go. Grudgingly. Unwillingly. Telling himself that he must not do this, that it must stop.

But as he pulled away from her his arm grazed the side of her breast and she let out a low moan.

It broke down the last of his self-control. His mouth was on hers again and before he realized what he was doing his hand was cupping her breast.

Sarah felt herself drowning in a sea of new and exhilarating experiences. But when his fingers brushed her soft and sensitive flesh she was suddenly shocked back into her senses. The intimate contact was so unknown to her, so completely beyond her experience, that she was afraid; afraid of the overpowering nature of her feelings and afraid of the intoxicating sensations they produced; and afraid of her feelings which were out of control.

She took a step back to distance herself from him but there was a tree directly behind her. She stood there for a moment, chest heaving, looking up at the insanely attractive man before her.

For a few tense seconds she almost succeeded in stepping aside and running back to the Grange. But she couldn't take the step. Because she didn't want to take it. What she wanted was to feel James's mouth on hers; what she wanted was to feel his hands on her body; what she wanted was to feel his hardened flesh pressing against her own. Her senses were reeling and she could think of nothing but the smouldering fire in his eyes, nothing but the heat of his body, nothing but the man in front of her; nothing but James.

She spread her hands against the tree behind her, bracing herself for she knew not what, and then with one throaty cry of 'Sarah!' he closed the distance between them, forcing her back against the tree as his hot mouth opened over hers.

Her body arced forwards and it drove him mad with desire. He kissed her again, sending shivers of ecstasy down her spine.

His mouth slid down to her throat, and she felt a bolt of exhilaration shoot through her . . .

to be followed by a wave of almost unbearable frustration as, with a strangled cry, he wrenched himself away and stepping back he said, 'What am I doing?'

Sarah looked at his horror-stricken face and felt her heart turn to stone.

He regretted it.

He wished he had never touched her.

Her heart and body, her spirit and mind, had been soaring with ecstasy, but he was horrified at what had just happened.

With a sick feeling twisting inside her she stumbled away from him, shame and humiliation overwhelming her as she picked up her skirts and ran back through the woodlands, back to the house.

The act of running helped to calm her overwrought emotions and on drawing near the terrace she slowed her step. It would not do for her to be seen running in from the gardens.

At the bottom of the steps she took a few minutes to steady herself. Although she intended to go straight to her room she would have to walk through the house to get there, and she did not want Lord Randall's many guests to realize she was distressed.

She breathed deeply, taking in the cool night air. It was fresh and calming.

How could she have let it happen?

How could she have lost all control?

Because so strong were her feelings for him

that when she had been in his arms nothing else had mattered. Nothing at all.

Gradually her pulse began to slow, until at last she felt equal to walking through the house. She went slowly up the steps, stopping for a moment at the top before going across the terrace and inside. Fortunately Lord Randall's guests were too busy enjoying themselves to take any notice of her, and she was able to make her way through the ballroom, across the hall and up the stairs to her own room.

Once inside she sank gratefully down on to her bed. The evening had been so eventful she needed some time to herself. What had been the meaning of James's look of horror?

Unfortunately it was all too obvious, she thought as she remembered the way he had forbidden Dominic to marry Miss Yardley. In a moment of madness he had given way to his feelings for her, but then his pride had reasserted itself and he had been horrified at what he had done. Horrified he had given way to his feelings for a governess. Horrified he had forgotten that she was beneath him, as Miss Yardley had been beneath his friend.

Well, if that was the case, then she would be a fool to break her heart over him, she told herself, her own pride coming to her aid. He was leaving the Grange on business the following day, once his guests had departed, and when he was gone everything would return to normal. She would settle down once again to teaching the children, and everything would be the way it was.

Or so she tried to tell herself.

She sighed, and began to get ready for bed. She was weary. The emotional strain of the evening had taken its toll and she wanted nothing more than to escape into oblivion for a few hours. Tomorrow everything would look brighter.

At least that was what she hoped.

*　　*　　*

Sarah woke early the following morning. She had fallen into an exhausted sleep as soon as her head had touched the pillow and she was now feeling much refreshed. The sound of the birds singing called her outdoors and dressing quickly, she slipped downstairs and went outside.

The air was cool, and she was glad of her shawl, but already it held the promise of another fine day.

As she made her way round to the stables, from where she could join one of the gravel paths that led through the shrubbery, she was pleased to find herself alone. It was too early for Lord Randall or his guests to be up; only the servants were stirring, preparing for another busy day.

The stable hands would be particularly busy,

seeing to horses and carriages, as Lord Randall's guests took their leave, and already they were up and about, but too absorbed to pay any attention to Sarah. She was just about to pass them by when Dixon, the head groom, looked round, and said, 'Here's Miss Davenport now.'

He was talking to a strange gentleman, who turned his attention to Sarah.

'Miss Davenport?' he asked.

'Yes.' Sarah looked at the man curiously. She did not know him, but decided that he looked like a secretary or a clerk.

'My name is Dodd, Miss Davenport. I'm sorry to have to tell you this, but your uncle has met with an accident. Your brother has sent me to fetch you home.'

CHAPTER ELEVEN

'Gone?' demanded Lord Randall later that morning. 'What do you mean, she's gone?'

He was in his study, having a brief respite from bidding his guests farewell, and a cold feeling gripped his insides as Hodgess informed him that Sarah had gone.

What had prompted him to overstep the bounds of propriety so completely the night before he did not know. It was not lust. He had experienced lust before, but he had never let it control his actions. And, no matter how strongly he was attracted to Sarah, it was not simply desire. It was a new emotion, something he had never felt before, some mixture of admiration, respect, friendship, attraction, protectiveness and tenderness that was entirely new to him.

Whatever it was, it had almost driven him to seduce her. The horror he had felt when he had realized that he was about to ruin an innocent young virgin—a horror that had appeared clearly on his face—had been enough to restore his sanity and make him back away, rescuing the situation before things got completely out of control.

He had wanted to go after her, to soothe the look of shock he had seen on her face, but no sooner had he broken free of the woodland than Mrs Cartwright and her daughter Annabelle had found him. To have gone after Sarah would have created a scandal—and how lucky he had been that Mrs Cartwright and her daughter had not seen Sarah fleeing in distress, he thought, or news of it would have run through the party like wildfire—and so he had had to let her go. And as soon as he had managed to extricate himself from Mrs Cartwright's attentions—to say nothing of Annabelle's simperings—he had been claimed by Mr Beveridge. In the end, he had had to console himself with the thought that he would be able to speak to Sarah first thing in the morning.

But the following morning she was nowhere to be found.

He had thought at first she must be sleeping late, exhausted by the emotional turmoil of the night before, and so he had turned his attention to his guests, bidding them a polite farewell. But by mid-morning, when most of them had left, and when he had still not seen anything of Sarah, he had asked Hodgess to find her. Only to be told that she had left the Grange.

The news hit him with unexpected force.

Hodgess cleared his throat nervously. 'Miss Davenport has left the Grange, my lord.'

James stared at him in disbelief.

'When?' he demanded. 'Why?' How?' The questions were fired rapidly, one after another, at the poor butler, who stood visibly quaking before him.

Have I driven her away? thought James, a cold feeling gripping him.

Have I frightened her with my love-making? But even as he thought it he dismissed the idea. Sarah's response to him had been innocent, but it had been decidedly passionate. Then why—and where—had she gone?

'She left early this morning, my lord,' trembled Hodgess.

'Why?' demanded Lord Randall again.

'It was on account of a message she received, my lord.'

'From whom?'

'From her brother, my lord.'

James looked amazed. Then, collecting his thoughts, he said, 'I think you had better tell me all about it. Starting at the beginning.'

'Yes, my lord. Very good, my lord,' said Hodgess. He stood there helplessly for a minute as though unsure how to begin, before at last taking the plunge. 'Well, my lord,' he said. 'It was like this. A carriage arrived early this morning—'

A private carriage?'

'Yes, my lord. A very fine equipage.'

'And the occupant? He was Miss Davenport's brother?'

'Oh, no, my lord, it wasn't her brother in the carriage. It was her brother's secretary. A Mr Dodd, my lord. He had an urgent message for Miss Davenport.'

'It *must* have been urgent, if the carriage arrived early this morning,' James said thoughtfully. 'Dodd must have travelled through the night.'

'Indeed, my lord.'

'And so Miss Davenport came to see me, my lord, and told me she was compelled to leave the Grange. Her uncle had met with an accident, she said, and she did not know when she would be able to return.'

'And you did not think of informing me?' Lord Randall demanded.

'It was early, my lord,' said Hodgess

uncomfortably. He had intended to inform his lordship of what had happened at once; it was not up to governesses, in Hodgess's opinion, to go gallivanting across the country at the drop of a hat, whatever the circumstances. But then the thought of rousing Lord Randall from his bed had proved too much for him and he had decided to say nothing until his lordship had seen his guests on their way.

'Miss Davenport has gone to her uncle, then. And he lives in . . .?'

Hodgess looked blank.

'Well, where had the carriage come from?'

'I'm sure I don't know, my lord,' said Hodgess. 'It wasn't my place to ask.'

James closed his eyes with frustration. Still, it was no use getting angry with Hodgess. The man had done his best. He opened them again.

'Of course it wasn't. Very well, Hodgess,' he said.

'Miss Davenport did say she would write,' volunteered Hodgess. 'Once she knew how long she would be away.'

At that moment the door opened and Lord Brancaster walked into the room.

'Not now, Brancaster,' said James, barely able to be civil because of his shock over Sarah's departure.

Young Lord Brancaster fingered his collar nervously but nevertheless stood his ground.

'I'm sorry, Randall. I know you're busy saying goodbye to your guests, but I have something important to say—something that can't wait. The thing is, Randall . . .' he went red. 'It's about Miss Leatherhead.'

'Miss Leatherhead?' James looked at him in astonishment.

'Yes.' Lord Brancaster took a deep breath. 'I know you're keen on her, Randall, and I don't blame you. She's an absolute angel. In fact, her mama warned me you were on the brink of making her a proposal. But the thing is, Randall . . .' He took another deep breath. 'We're in love.'

'In love?' James asked blankly. His mind was too full of Sarah for him to be able to take in what Lord Brancaster was saying.

'Yes.' Lord Brancaster sounded more definite now. 'In love. The thing is, Randall,' he said, summoning his courage, 'you're too old for her. Margaret's only just turned twenty, and you're . . . well, I shouldn't be saying this, but . . .'

James gave a broad grin. He was by now giving Lord Brancaster his full attention, and he had the feeling that one of his problems was going to be solved for him in a most agreeable way.

'Of course you should, Brancaster. Go on.'

'Well . . . you're in your thirties, damn it!' Lord Brancaster, at that moment looking much younger than his twenty-five years, exploded. 'I know we've served you an ill turn . . . or I have. It wasn't Margaret's fault. I am the one to blame. But the fact of the matter is I've asked her to marry me and she's said yes.'

'And what do her parents have to say about it?' asked James.

'We haven't told them yet,' Lord Brancaster admitted. 'But I'm a rich man, and a titled one. If they knew you wouldn't cut up rough about it, Margaret thinks they'd be happy to agree.'

James clapped Lord Brancaster on the back.

'I'm sincerely delighted for you,' he said. 'You're right. I am too old for Margaret. I wish you joy, Brancaster. You and Margaret both.'

'Really?' Lord Brancaster let out a sigh of relief. 'And here was I thinking you'd cut up rough! I must go and tell Margaret. Thank you, Randall.'

And with that he made a bow and left the room.

If only all my problems could be solved so easily, thought James as he watched him go.

But they could not, and he found himself wondering, agonizingly, how long it would be before he saw Sarah again.

*   *   *

Sarah was at that minute sitting in her uncle's carriage, heading towards Bath.

She had at first been torn on receiving her brother's message. She was sorry to be leaving the children, but her common sense reminded her that the boys still had their tutors and that Lucy still had her nurse; she knew they would be well looked after in her absence.

And James. What of James? Her feelings for him were too painful to dwell on. It was fortunate, she told herself, that she had been called away from the Grange. By the time she returned James would have left—he was, she knew, going to attend to some business in London—and she would therefore not have to see him. It was a lucky solution, she told herself.

She turned her thoughts away from James and back to her brother's urgent message. Once she had received it she had stayed only long enough to pack a valise and let Hodgess know what had happened, and had then set out with Mr Dodd. As yet she did not know the nature of her uncle's accident, but knew she would learn more as soon as she arrived.

At last the carriage rumbled to a halt. The step was let down, Sarah stepped out and stood before the magnificent house in Laura Place, home to her aunt and uncle; and, since her father's death, home to her brothers as well.

'Sarah!'

Almost as soon as she entered the hall Nicholas was there, embracing her and asking after her journey.

The house was just as she remembered it, being richly and expensively furnished:

marble-topped console tables, gilded mirrors and antique vases brought back by her uncle from his Grand Tour vied with family portraits, elegant water-colours and a number of shield-backed chairs.

And Nicholas. Nicholas was still Nicholas, her good-tempered, handsome brother; although he looked older and more capable than the last time she had seen him, over a year before.

But she had no time for further observation: she was too anxious to discover what had happened.

'How is my uncle?' she asked him as he helped her off with her pelisse. 'Is he badly hurt?'

He turned to Mr Dodd. 'Thank you, Dodd,' he said. 'That will be all. I think you'd better prepare yourself,' he said to Sarah as he led her into the drawing-room. 'I'm afraid Uncle Hugh has had a fall. He's been drinking heavily for years now, and it was only a matter of time before something like this happened. Still, it was a terrible shock.'

'You mean . . .?'

Nicholas nodded. 'Unfortunately the accident was fatal. Uncle Hugh broke his neck.'

Sarah heaved a sigh. Her uncle had never been kind to her, but he should have had another ten years of life left to him and she was sorry he was dead.

'How has my aunt taken it? Is she very distressed?'

'On the surface, yes—she loves to be the centre of attention. But underneath, no. There was no love lost between them; they had hardly spoken a civilized word in years.'

Sarah nodded. Although her aunt and uncle had always been far wealthier than her parents, they had not been nearly as happy.

'She has spent the day with her dressmakers,' went on Nicholas, 'ordering a whole new wardrobe of mourning clothes. And quite the most stylish—and expensive—mourning clothes they will be.' He gave a grimace. 'But never mind Aunt Claire. It's you I want to talk about, Sarah. Now that my uncle is dead, I am the new Lord Craden, and my first act as Lord Craden is to ask you to come and live here.' His face crinkled into a smile. 'I've spent the last year racking my brains, trying to think of a way of providing for you. I couldn't bear the thought of your having to work for your living. Especially as a governess. But now your days of hardship are over.'

'No, Nick, I can't do that. I can't just abandon the children. Besides, my aunt will object.'

'It won't do any good if she does,' said Nicholas. 'It's no longer her decision. And as for leaving the children—I know you're attached to them, Sarah, but when you've had time to think about it you'll realize it isn't suitable for you to continue being a governess. Don't worry, Lord Randall will find someone else to look after them. But now I want to talk about you. The one thought that has kept me going through this awful day is the thought that at last you will be provided for as you should be. We'll have to live quietly at first, of course, whilst we're in mourning, but after that I mean to make sure you have fun. I mean to take you to concerts and the theatre and escort you to any number of balls.'

'The last thing I'm thinking about now is dancing,' sighed Sarah. Her mind was in a whirl. So much had happened in the last twenty-four hours that she was still trying to make sense of it all.

Nicholas nodded. 'You must be tired after your journey. I've had a room prepared for you. Rest for as long as you like. I'll make sure no one disturbs you.'

Sarah kissed him lightly on the cheek.

'Listen to you, taking charge,' she said affectionately. 'You've grown up a lot since the last time I saw you, Nicholas.'

He nodded. 'But it's thanks to the good upbringing you gave Geoffrey and me after mother died.'

She smiled. 'Flatterer!' she said.

'Make the most of it,' he joked. 'The flattery lasts for one night only. Tomorrow I'll be back to putting spiders in your bed!'

*   *   *

Although the days until the funeral were full ones for Sarah she found that, disturbingly, her thoughts were never far away from James. Why she persisted in thinking of him she did not know: his expression had made it quite clear what his feelings were and she told herself repeatedly that he was not worth the pain she felt. Perhaps things would be easier when she had made good on her promise and had written to him, she thought. After all, it was difficult to forget about him when she knew she still had the letter to write. Perhaps, once that painful task was done she would be better able to put him out of her mind.

But it was not an easy letter to write. How should she word it? What should she say?

She gathered her thoughts. She needed to let him know that her uncle had died and that her brother had succeeded to the title; needed to tell him, too, that her place now was with her family and that, however much she would miss the children, she could not return to the Grange.

Nicholas was right, she thought. I cannot go on being a governess, and although the children will miss me to begin with they will in time adjust to someone else.

But where to start?

She pulled a sheet of paper towards her and began:

My lord . . .

She put down her quill: she was finding it difficult to write to him in such cold terms after all they had shared. But it must be done. What they had shared had meant nothing to him. She was lucky, then, that fate had given her a way out of an impossible situation, she told herself.

But why then did she still feel pain?

She shook her head. This was not getting her letter to Lord Randall done. She picked up her quill again. Bit by bit she began to write, composing the letter slowly and with difficulty, but at last it was done. She was just adding the direction when Nicholas entered the room.

'Writing to someone, Sis?' he asked.

'To Lord Randall,' she told him briefly as she shook sand over the letter to dry the ink.

Nicholas gave a broad grin and whisked the sheet of paper from the escritoire. 'No need to do that, Sarah. I wrote to Randall this morning and told him you wouldn't be coming back.'

'Nick!' Sarah was horrified. 'You had no business doing anything of the kind.'

'Why ever not?' Nicholas was mystified. 'You're finished with governessing, Sarah. And a good thing too. When I think of what you had to put up with at the hands of that proud, arrogant monster . . .' he said, remembering Sarah's early, unflattering letters from the Grange.

'He was never a monster,' Sarah returned.

'Of course he was, or you wouldn't have taken against him. You've never been quick to judge people, Sarah, but you said—'

'I know what I said,' she flushed, 'but—'

'—that he was the most proud and disagreeable man you had ever met in your life,' Nicholas continued, not to be put off. 'Those were your very words.'

'To begin with, perhaps,' said Sarah, wondering confusedly why she was defending him, 'but when I got to know him he wasn't like that at all. He is a proud man, but he isn't disagreeable.'

'Still, that part of your life is over now,' said Nicholas with a shrug. 'You're back with your family. Where you belong.'

Sarah sighed. It was no use her trying to explain to Nicholas that her feelings for James had undergone a complete transformation since her early letters from the Grange. In fact, she realized, there was no point. James did not love her—for if he had loved her he would not have been horrified that he had kissed her; that he had kissed a *governess*—and no matter how much it hurt her she had to acknowledge that what Nick said was true. That part of her life was over; and over for good.

Even so, she was determined to send her letter. She had promised to send one and send one she would. She waited only for Nicholas to leave the room before finishing writing the direction and seeing that it went in the post.

And then she sat down to write to the children. She did not want them to feel she had abandoned them, and wrote them a long and lively letter, reassuring them of her affection for them whilst explaining in simple terms that, as her uncle had died, she would not be able to return to the Grange.

*   *   *

'The stable doors are rotten and need replacing.' James's voice was curt. 'I want them seeing to at once.'

'Yes, my lord. Right away, my lord,' said the estate carpenter.

'And when you're finished, the floorboards in the tack-room need attention. They have cracked with the heat. See what you can do with them.'

'Yes, my lord. Very good, my lord,' said Higgins again.

And what's eating him? he thought, as he backed his way out of Lord Randall's study.

Although always high-handed, Lord Randall had become even worse since the house-party—and just when Higgins and all the rest of the servants had been looking forward to a rest. Lord Randall had informed them that he would be leaving the Grange once the party was over, and they had thought they would have a chance to catch their breath. But he had changed his mind at the last minute and was still at the Grange.

Higgins could not know, none of the servants could, that James's temper was so short because he had not heard from Sarah since she had left the Grange in such a hurry almost a week before, and that he had changed his plans to leave the Grange because he wanted to be there when the promised letter from Sarah arrived.

To begin with he had been patient, but as the days had passed and no letter had arrived his patience had worn extremely thin. Nothing had been able to hold his attention. Not even the news that Farbey was indeed the Radical ringleader. At one time such important news would have meant so much to him, especially as he had spent months tracking down the leader of the Radical group. But the news that Farbey had been arrested before he could do any real harm, and was now languishing in prison, meant nothing to him. The only thing that mattered to him was Sarah's absence. That one fact dominated his life.

The door opened and Hodgess entered the room.

'The mail has arrived, my lord. You asked to be informed.'

'Yes. Very good, Hodgess. Send it in.'

A minute later the mail appeared on a silver salver. James glanced briefly at the top three letters and then studied the fourth. He did not recognize the hand but . . . Curiously, he broke the seal, to be rewarded by his first news of Sarah for a week. The letter was from her brother, and was curt almost to the point of rudeness. But James did not care about that. All he cared about was knowing that Sarah was safe and happy, and that she would soon be returning to the Grange. But as he read the letter his brow darkened. Never coming back? He read the words in disbelief. It couldn't be true. Sarah, never coming back to the Grange?

He dropped his hand to his side, still holding the letter, and looked sightlessly out of the window. She must come back. She had to come back. He needed her, wanted her . . . loved her.

He let out an explosive sigh. Yes, he loved her. How could he have been so blind? How could he have denied his feelings simply because she was a governess? What did it matter? She might not be his equal in rank, but she was his equal in everything that mattered, in heart, spirit and mind. And he must tell her so. Tell her his feelings, offer her his heart and his hand.

He rang for the butler.

'Send a message to the stables. Tell them I want the carriage ready in half an hour. Oh, and Hodgess, inform Mrs Smith that I will not be in for dinner tonight. I am going to Bath.'

* * *

Sarah's days settled into a regular pattern in Bath. In the morning she saw to the household, and in the afternoons she accompanied her aunt to the Pump Room. Although the family was in mourning Aunt Claire had refused to give up her visits to the Pump Room, and had persuaded her tame physician, Dr Henner, to order her to take the waters. She insisted that Sarah must go with her to lend her an arm if she should feel fatigued. 'For my nerves have had a terrible shock,' she said, 'and if I don't take care, I will follow my poor dear Hugh to an early grave.'

Sarah did not object to this arrangement. She felt that she must do what she could to put the past behind her and embark on a new life. She owed it to her brothers, especially Nicholas, who often expressed his concern about her listless spirits.

The Pump Room was the source of much of the social life of Bath. Here people went to drink the waters which they hoped would bring them good health. Here, too, people went to gossip, and Sarah's aunt liked nothing better than to while away the time by talking to her friends, whilst pretending that she was only there to satisfy Dr Henner.

'For myself,' she said hypocritically to Mrs Fenella Lovatt, 'I would much rather stay at home. But Dr Henner insists, and I am much too weak to argue with him.'

'My dear Claire, you must do *exactly* as your

physician says,' commanded Mrs Lovatt. She had few friends in Bath, particularly at this time of year when it was almost empty of visitors, and she was not prepared to lose Claire's company over such a thing as the death of a drunken husband. 'We can't have you fading away, my dear. You must keep your strength up. You owe it to the memory of your poor, dear Hugh.'

Leaving her aunt to gossip, Sarah took a turn about the room. It was large and airy, with a high ceiling and a viewing gallery at one end. Fine columns ornamented the walls and large windows flooded the room with light. For the most part the Pump Room was empty, but here and there small groups of people gathered together to pass the time of day.

'Looking a bit peaky this morning, Miss Davenport,' came a bluff, hearty voice at her side.

Sarah turned to see Major Weatherspoon, one of the residents of Bath. With his large, bulbous nose and his florid complexion, to say nothing of his rotund figure, he always reminded Sarah—in the nicest possible way—of an overgrown gnome.

'Better try a glass of the waters,' he went on, with a twinkle in his kindly old eyes. 'Young girls like you shouldn't be looking peaky—not unless they've been crossed in love!'

This remark was a little too close for comfort, and Sarah made an effort to appear animated. She did not want her low spirits to occasion gossip.

'Can't come to the Pump Room and not take the waters,' he said jovially. Without more ado he fetched her a glass. 'Smells bad and tastes worse!' He gave her a wink. 'That's why it does you good!'

Sarah smiled and took the glass. She liked Major Weatherspoon, and who knew? The waters might indeed help her to recover her spirits.

She lifted the glass to her lips. She was just about to drink when some instinct told her to turn towards the door. For some strange reason she had the feeling that James was there. It was ridiculous, and yet . . .

She turned, and what she saw made the colour rise to her cheeks. There, talking to a cluster of people by the door, was James.

He looked magnificent; stronger and more virile than ever. His tanned skin was accentuated by the snowiness of his linen, and his black eyes danced with warmth and light. His broad shoulders filled his superbly cut tail-coat, and his long, firm legs gave his breeches a smooth finish, before they disappeared into top boots that, highly polished, shone in the light.

Her heart leapt. But then her common sense reasserted itself. What a misfortune, to meet him here, in Bath.

But of course. She had known he intended

to leave the Grange after the house-party and once he had attended to his business, why should he not visit the fashionable spa?

Major Weatherspoon, seeing her flush, looked at her curiously, then followed her gaze.

'Handsome fella, Randall,' he said. 'Just arrived this morning. Staying at the White Hart, by all accounts. Good place, the White Hart. Good food and the sheets always properly aired. D'you know him, m'dear?'

Sarah made a supreme effort to bring her emotions under control.

Seeing James in Bath, when she had imagined him to be in London, had nearly undone her, but she took herself in hand, telling herself that, although it might be difficult for her to meet James, it was something she must school herself to do.

Now that she had been restored to her rightful position in society she would no doubt come across him in places such as London and Bath, and, no matter what her feelings might be, she must be able to meet him without appearing to be unsettled.

He may be high-handed and arrogant, he may have pulled away from her in horror when he had realized he had given way to his feelings for a governess, and it may have caused her terrible pain. But she must not allow any of this to show. She must treat him in the same way she would have treated him if there had never been anything between them; she, too, had her pride.

'We've met,' she replied coolly. She was pleased to hear that her voice was level, without any hint of a tremble.

'Good for you, m'dear,' said Major Weatherspoon jovially. 'Well, mustn't monopolize you. But if you don't want to drink the stuff,' he added conspiratorially, looking at her glass, 'put it in the corner.' He glanced towards one side of the room where two or three glasses had already been left. Then, with a last wink, he strolled away.

James, who had been watching Sarah from the moment he entered the room, saw the old man leaving her. Making his excuses to the people he was talking to he crossed the room, his eyes fixed on hers.

Seeing him striding towards her made Sarah's treacherous body react as it had always done when he was near, sending shivers up her arms and down her spine. Surely she could not still have feelings for him, after their last disastrous encounter?

His face broke into a smile.

'Sarah,' he said. 'At last!' He looked at her with a profound sense of satisfaction. 'I've found you.'

His greeting was so warm that her instinct was to return his greeting with an equally warm one of her own. But no. She would not betray herself in that way.

‘Lord Randall,’ she replied in a voice that was firm and cool.

He looked puzzled at the coolness of her manner. Whatever Sarah had been in the past, she had never been cool. But knowing that her uncle had just died he put it down to her recent bereavement.

Sarah, finding that he did not simply make some polite comment about the weather and then move on, felt compelled to fill the awkward silence. Presumably he felt it would not be polite of him to ignore her, and wanted to accord her the same courtesy he would accord any other young lady of his acquaintance.

‘How long have you been in Bath, my lord?’ she asked.

It was a polite and formal sentence, correct in every way, but it was totally unlike Sarah. She seemed so different that for one disconcerting moment James felt that he was talking to a stranger.

‘Is something wrong?’ he said, taking her by the shoulders and looking down into her face with concern. ‘There is, isn’t there? Won’t you tell me what it is?’

‘We are in a public place,’ she said. ‘People will stare.’ She shrugged away from him, unable to bear his touch. It awakened too many memories.

‘Since when have you been worried about what other people think?’ he asked her, concerned at her changed manner. 'You have always done and said exactly what you needed to do and say, without regard to convention. What's happened, Sarah?'

It was a question to which he never received an answer, for at that moment Sarah's Aunt Claire, having seen that Sarah was speaking to a personable—and obviously wealthy—man, had decided to join her.

'Why, Sarah, my dear,' she said with deceptive sweetness, 'I am sorry to have kept you so long. It really is trying to have to visit the Pump Room every day, but Dr Henner will insist I take the waters. I hope you have not been too bored?'

'That's quite all right, Aunt Claire,' said Sarah. She was pleased, for once, to be interrupted by her aunt. She was finding it difficult to treat James with the cool but polite manner she had decided would best suit the situation, and was glad of an opportunity to bring the chance meeting—as she thought of it—to an end. 'It has been a pleasure to meet you again, Lord Randall.' She turned to go.

James's brow darkened. For some reason he could not understand Sarah was being distant, but he did not intend to leave until he had found out what it was. She was clearly not going to give him any help at the moment, however, and so he turned to her aunt instead.

'The waters here are said to be very good. Have you found them effective?'

Sarah frowned. She had expected him to be as pleased as she was that the awkward situation they had found themselves in had been so easily resolved. But instead he seemed determined to prolong the encounter. Why, she did not know.

Her treacherous heart hoped for one minute that she had been mistaken about his reaction in the woodland; that he was genuinely pleased to see her; but common sense told her that there was a more likely reason for his attention. Finding himself in Bath, and unexpectedly seeing her there, he had most probably decided to make the most of the opportunity to talk to her about the children and ask her advice, perhaps, on appointing a new governess.

Yes, that would explain it. And of course she would give him every help she could in that direction.

Even so, she was not at ease. Conflicting emotions were at war within her: joy at seeing James again; anger at his pride; contempt for his rejection of her in the woodland; and bewilderment at his evident desire to be with her again.

Her aunt, however, was in her element.

'Most effective,' Aunt Claire said, in answer to James's question; whilst thinking: I hope Fenella is watching this. She will be *green* with envy. 'How I could have got through these last few weeks without them I do not know . . .'

As her aunt's voice flowed on, Sarah became increasingly uncomfortable. If he wanted to ask her advice on something concerning the children, why did he not do so? Instead of listening to Aunt Claire's every word, and saying, when her aunt at last revealed that they were about to return to Laura Place:

'Perhaps you will allow me to escort you there?'

'That is most kind,' replied her aunt, taking his proffered arm.

He offered his other arm to Sarah. She swallowed. There was nothing for it. She would have to take it. She rested her hand on his arm so lightly that she was barely touching him, but it was enough to reawaken all her physical feelings for him. What a stroke of bad luck it had been, meeting him in the Pump Room, she thought, without realizing that he had come there on purpose to find her.

'How I wish I could take a turn in the Spring Gardens,' Aunt Claire sighed as they returned to the elegant town house in Laura Place. 'It is such a beautiful day. But alas! I don't have the strength.'

'Then we will take a turn there together,' said James.

'What a splendid notion!' Aunt Claire replied, as though the idea had never occurred to her.

Sarah's tension increased. Surely it wasn't

necessary for James to prolong their chance encounter like this?

Once in the Spring Gardens, Sarah's tension increased still further because, saying to Aunt Claire that she must not tire herself, James settled that lady down on a seat and then continued to walk on with Sarah alone. Never far from Aunt Claire; she was still obviously Sarah's chaperon; but far enough for their conversation not to be overheard.

As soon as it was possible Sarah detached her hand from his arm. The feelings it produced were clouding her mind, and that was already confused enough.

'It was very kind of you to see my aunt and myself safely home, Lord Randall,' she said. 'But now I believe we must detain you no longer.'

'Why didn't you write to me, Sarah?' Now that they were alone he went to the heart of the matter straight away. 'I waited for a letter but it never came. All I had was a letter from your brother telling me that you were never returning to the Grange.'

She was surprised at his concern. She had expected him to be relieved that such a difficult situation had, by chance, been resolved so easily.

He looked down at her with tender concern. She was looking tired, he thought. Seeing a bench close beside them he held out his hands and invited her to sit down.

She hesitated for a moment and then reluctantly agreed. She had had a chance now to let his words sink in, and if he thought she had not written to him as she had promised to do, then it was not altogether surprising that he should want an explanation.

'If you are in difficulties of some kind . . .' he began. He knew that her uncle had died, as Nicholas had told him so in his letter, but he also knew she had never been close to her uncle, and he was growing increasingly sure that it was not her bereavement that had caused her distant manner.

'You didn't get my letter?' she asked.

'No.'

'But you have heard from Nicholas?'

'Yes. As soon as I'd read his letter I set out for Bath.'

'My letter was closely following it. You must have left before it arrived. But you read Nicholas's letter, you say, and set out at once for Bath?'

'Of course. I had to find you.'

She felt a new warmth stealing over her. 'Then you came here on purpose to find me?' There was a note of hope in her voice. Could it be possible that he had wanted to see her again? That she had been mistaken about the look of horror that had crossed his face in the woodlands? She hardly dared hope.

'If you've read my brother's letter then you know why I can't come back to the Grange. I don't *want* to leave the children,' she said, this being safe ground to tread on—far safer than revealing that she did not want to leave James—'but I can no longer be a governess and—'

'I don't want you to come back as a governess,' he interrupted. As he looked into her eyes, her sea-green eyes, he could not believe it had taken him so long to realize the depth of his feelings for her. But now that he had realized he loved her he wanted to waste no more time. He took her hands in his and a warm smile spread over his face.

Sarah felt her spirits lift. The touch of his hand was so magical, the look in his eyes so warm and sincere, that her impossible dream seemed real. She felt the breath catch in her throat.

'Sarah,' he said, his smile softening his whole face. 'I want you to come back as my wife.'

It is a dream, she thought. It can't be true.

Seeing her dazed expression he said, 'Are you really so surprised? Sarah, my life is empty without you. I didn't realize how much I need you until you had gone. It shouldn't have taken your brother's letter to make me see it,' he went on, remembering how it was the news that Sarah would not be returning that had finally made him acknowledge the true nature of his feelings for her, 'but once I had read it I knew I must make you my wife . . .'

He stopped. A strange expression had come over Sarah's face. At the moment he had mentioned her brother's letter, something had changed.

'It was the letter that decided you?' she asked in an uncertain voice.

'Yes,' he smiled.

'I see.' Her tone was lifeless.

He looked at her, puzzled. 'You see?'

'Yes. I see.'

'Would you care to explain that remark?' he asked, curious.

'I think I would rather not.' Her voice was now as hard as stone.

'I think you must.' He had the disturbing feeling that the young lady in front of him was a stranger, and that the open, warm-hearted person he had fallen in love with was no longer there. Her manner was so different from her honest and outspoken manner at the Grange that he felt he was talking to someone he had never met before.

'Very well, then,' she said, turning to look him directly in the eye. 'I see that you only decided to offer me your hand once you discovered that I was no longer a lowly governess, but was instead the sister of a baron.'

'A baron?' he echoed in astonishment. Nicholas's letter had mentioned nothing of that.

'Or do you mean to pretend that you didn't

know?' she asked rashly, too hurt, angry and disillusioned to ask herself what Nicholas had actually put in his letter, and to consider whether her accusation was just.

His face darkened.

'And this is your estimation of my character?' he asked, his eyes looking deeply into her own as though he could read the answer there. 'You believe I could be swayed by such a mean consideration?'

'Do you deny it?' she demanded, remembering the look of horror on his face in the woodland, and remembering, too, the way in which he had prevented his friend from making an unequal marriage.

He looked at her searchingly for another minute and then his expression changed to one of contempt.

'What is the point?' he demanded. 'You have already made up your mind. I will not demean myself by rebutting such an absurd suggestion, even if you can demean yourself by making it. I never thought anything could change you, Sarah, but you *have* changed. Your good fortune, instead of improving you, has destroyed your open and honest nature and made you cold, hard and cynical. I wish you joy of your new-found position—and your new-found personality. And as for my proposal,' he went on, his arrogance hiding the deep hurt that was threatening to consume him at the discovery that Sarah had apparently changed beyond recognition, 'pray do not trouble yourself to give me an answer. I see now it is repugnant to you, and I assure you that in this matter, if no other, we think as one.'

And with a look of disgust that left Sarah seething he strode away from her.

How could he have twisted everything, making it appear that she was the one who was in the wrong? *You believe I could be swayed by such a mean consideration* indeed! Of course she believed he could be swayed by such a mean consideration, because it was exactly that consideration that had led him to forbid Dominic to marry Miss Yardley, she thought; little realizing that Miss Yardley, as well as being from a new and unconnected family, was ignorant and vulgar as well.

She turned on her heel and, eyes blazing, returned to her aunt.

'But where is Lord Randall?' asked Aunt Claire.

'Lord Randall was unavoidably called away,' said Sarah shortly. She was certainly not going to furnish her aunt with any clearer explanation; she had no intention of letting her affairs form the main substance of her aunt's next session of gossip.

'That is most unfortunate,' grumbled her aunt. 'I was so hoping that Lady Harmon would notice him as we walked past her window.'

'Lady Harmon will just have to be disappointed,' retorted Sarah.

'Ah, well,' said Aunt Claire. 'He may be the first, but he certainly won't be the last. You are a baron's sister now, Sarah. You will soon have a great many young men falling at your feet.'

Leaving Sarah to wonder why, when she herself had accused James of being influenced by her new station in life, she deeply resented her aunt for voicing the same opinion.

CHAPTER TWELVE

'There is a gentleman to see you, miss.'

It was the following morning, and Sarah was busy arranging fresh flowers in the drawing-room when the butler made the announcement.

'A gentleman?' asked Sarah.

Her heart missed a beat at the words, although outwardly she remained calm. She added another flower to the vase. 'Who is it, Hoskins?'

'The gentleman said you would know who it was, miss.'

'Did he, indeed?' she asked.

'Yes, miss.'

'In that case, you had better show him in.'

She was annoyed to find that her fingers trembled as she finished the arrangement.

After all that had passed between them on the previous day, why had James returned?

And why was she so pleased that he had?

Could it be because she hoped that he really had not known of her change of circumstances? That it had all been a horrible mistake?

She took a deep breath to steady herself and put a final flower in the vase as she heard the gentleman enter the room. But as she turned round she saw to her surprise that it was not James who was being ushered into the drawing-room. It was Mr Haversage.

She was so astonished that she could do no more than gasp, 'Mr Haversage,' whilst she adjusted herself to this unexpected visitor.

'And whom did you expect?' he asked, as he walked into the room with a swagger. He lifted his eyebrows. 'James?'

Sarah's expression hardened. She had been momentarily taken aback, but now she had had time to gather her wits and she went over to the bell.

'I wouldn't do that, if I were you,' he said. Sarah did not falter, and so he added, 'That is, if you wish to see Lucy again.'

Sarah stopped, surprised.

'What has Lucy to do with anything?' she asked. For one confused moment she wondered whether James had perhaps sent Mr Haversage to ask her to teach Lucy until he could find a replacement governess, but she quickly dismissed the idea as nonsensical. Leaving her to wonder how Mr Haversage had discovered her whereabouts, and what he was doing there.

'A great deal. May I?'

He indicated a chair.

Sarah did not want the man there, but she was curious. She was in no danger. One tug at the bell would bring a footman to her assistance. She gave a cold nod.

He sat down.

'We parted on bad terms,' he said. His manner was friendly, apologetic even. 'I don't like to be on bad terms with anyone, Sarah—'

'I have told you before. I don't think you should call me that.'

'My apologies. Miss Davenport,' he said.

Sarah did not reply. Even though he was being polite and friendly there was something about Mr Haversage that unsettled her. She felt the small hairs on the back of her neck rise and she wondered again what he was doing there.

Mr Haversage looked around the room. 'This is a pleasant house you have—or, should I say, your brother has. I heard about his good fortune—and yours. My own fortune, alas, has not been so good. There are so few opportunities open to a man of my talents. But all that is about to change.'

He took something out of the inside pocket of his coat and put it on the table.

Sarah looked at it in disbelief. It was a lock of Lucy's hair, still tied with the pink ribbon she had worn at the concert.

Her eyes flicked to his. 'Where did you get that?' she demanded.

'From Lucy's head, of course. Where else? Don't worry. The rest of her is in one piece—for now.'

Sarah felt cold fingers gripping at her insides. Her instincts were to ring the bell and have the servants take Mr Haversage in charge, but she didn't want to do anything to provoke him. At least not until she had discovered what was going on. She did not know what Mr Haversage had done, or what he might be capable of doing, but she did know from her own experience that he was dangerous. She had to find out how he had come by Lucy's lock of hair.

'Why have you come here?' she asked. She kept her voice calm and level.

He put his feet up on the exquisitely inlaid table. 'To claim my reward.'

'For what?' asked Sarah, trying not to show her surprise. Mr Haversage was unpredictable. He was also clearly unbalanced.

'Why, for finding Lucy, of course,' he said.

'Lucy isn't lost,' returned Sarah. But already she was beginning to have an uneasy feeling in the pit of her stomach.

'Of course she isn't,' he said smilingly. The smile was odd, deepening Sarah's unease.

'She's safe with me.'

'I don't see her.' Sarah looked around significantly.

'Not with me *here*,' he said, thrusting his hands into his trouser pockets and staring at the lock of hair. 'She's in a little cottage I have, just a few miles out of town.'

'You don't have a cottage,' remarked Sarah.

'*Didn't* have a cottage,' he corrected her. 'But, knowing that a large sum of money was coming my way—a very large sum of money—I decided to indulge myself. It is a *sweet* little cottage out in the country, in the fresh, clean air. Just the sort of place for a little girl to flourish.'

'I don't believe you.'

'Oh, don't you? Then how did I come by her hair?'

'You could have come by it in any number of ways,' replied Sarah. But she was growing more and more uneasy, and Mr Haversage sensed it.

'Then, if I don't have her, you don't have anything to worry about, do you? If, on the other hand, I *do* have her—well, then, that puts a different complexion on things. Don't you agree?'

Sarah did not reply.

'I'd say it does. To the tune of—oh, say, about twenty thousand pounds.'

'Twenty thousand pounds?' Sarah was astonished. 'You surely can't think I have that much money, and even—'

'Oh, but you do,' replied Mr Haversage smoothly. 'I have been making a few enquiries. It is the exact amount your brother has settled on you. News of it is all round town. But, of course, if Lucy's life isn't worth it . . .'

'If you really had Lucy you would have gone to Lord Randall, instead of coming to me,' said Sarah wisely. 'He could give you far more than twenty thousand pounds.'

'Go to a six foot two ex-soldier when I could go to a five foot six governess?' He laughed. 'I think not.' He stood up and held out his hand. 'Goodbye, Miss Davenport.' He gave her a smile. 'I don't expect we will meet again.'

His apparently normal manner was chilling; more chilling than an obviously mad manner would have been.

'You won't hurt Lucy,' Sarah said. 'You would be caught and punished. What's more, you are intelligent enough to know it.'

'Perhaps I would, and perhaps I wouldn't,' he said. 'But would it really be any consolation to you? Knowing that I was dead? If Lucy was too? But still, if you're not interested . . .'

He crossed the room, and had almost reached the door when Sarah said, 'Wait! If I am to give you money—any money—although I make no promises; but if I am to give you money then first of all I must have proof that you really do have Lucy.'

'You're not very trusting, are you?' he

asked. 'But then, you've no reason to be. Very well, then, if you want proof, you can come with me. I am going to Lucy now.'

'I can't come with you to an isolated cottage. It would be stupid.'

She was prolonging the conversation in order to buy herself time. Time to think of some kind of solution to the appalling problem that had presented itself.

'Not stupid,' he shrugged. 'Simply desperate.'

Sarah was thinking even as he spoke. If she did not go with Mr Haversage now she would have no chance of finding Lucy. But if she went alone she would be completely in his power. Nicholas, Geoffrey and Aunt Claire were out of the house, but even if they had been there her thoughts would still have turned to James. Much as she loved her brothers they were untried boys; James was a seasoned man. No matter how disgusted he had been with her the day before, no matter how angry, he would not fail her. And no matter how angry she had been with him she discovered that, in this way at least, she still had complete and utter faith in him.

But Mr Haversage was not going to let her send James a message, or indeed send a message to anyone else. And it would be useless to try and enlist the help of the servants. Even if they overpowered Mr Haversage they would not be able to force him to say where Lucy was.

Desperation sharpened her wits and an idea came to her. Speaking as though she was thinking aloud she shook her head and muttered, 'I can't go with him now . . .'

'In that case . . .' said Mr Haversage, making once more for the door.

'You don't understand,' she said out loud. 'I'm meant to be meeting James in an hour. If I don't turn up he'll know something is wrong.'

It was a lie, but Mr Haversage did not know that.

'So, of course, you will have to send him a message. And in this message you will just happen to mention that I have been here threatening Lucy?' He shook his finger at her. 'Oh, no, Sarah. You'll have to do better than that.' He smiled, pleased that he had seen through her plan.

But Sarah had never expected to solve the problem so simply. 'Then he will come here anyway. As soon as I don't turn up he will want to know what happened.'

Mr Haversage looked at her appraisingly. 'You think you've got it all sewn up, don't you? If I let you send a message you can warn James. And if I don't, he'll wonder what's wrong and come here to find out, discovering that you have left with me.' He smiled suddenly. 'It might be amusing to let James think you've chosen me after all. But I can't help thinking it would lead to complications.

So, instead, this is what you are going to do. You are going to write a note to James. But you are not going to have a chance to let him know what is going on. Because I am going to be looking over your shoulder and watching every word you write.'

Sarah did not allow her relief to show on her face. It was important that Mr Haversage should think he had spoiled her plan. That way, he would be off guard and not detect her real plan.

She made a show of resignation, then sat down at the desk.

Mr Haversage had been so pleased with himself for seeing through her ruse that it never occurred to him that her 'meeting' with James might not have been real. Leaving Sarah to hope that James would be able to see through the message she was able to send; a message that must let him know something was wrong without actually saying so.

There was one thing in her favour. Mr Haversage thought she was having an affair with James, and she could use that to her advantage.

Dipping one of the quill pens into the ink, she began.

My darling James

She paused, then went on.

I can't meet you for lunch as we arranged—my brother suspects that we are having an affair and has forbidden me to leave the house. I will be at Lady Jenson's soirée tomorrow evening—make sure you are there.
Don't fail me.

She signed it,

Yours for ever, Sarah.

The letter was gibberish, but Mr Haversage did not know that. James, however, would. The letter would perplex him, but she hoped that it would also tell him that something was wrong. And she knew James well enough to know that he would want an answer to the questions the message would raise.

'Very pretty,' smirked Mr Haversage. 'And to think Randall denied that you were having an affair. When did it begin, Sarah? After our little run-in at the ruins, or before?'

'Mind your own business,' she retorted sharply. If Mr Haversage was to believe the pretence she must behave as though she was having an affair with James.

'Very well,' he said. 'Now call the butler. I want to make sure this message will be delivered. And then we have a visit to make . . .'

* * *

At that moment James was angrily packing up his things as he prepared to leave Bath. He had come there to propose to Sarah, but any hope of a marriage between them was now over. Sarah had changed. The person he had fallen in love with no longer existed, and loath as he was to admit it, even to himself, the cause must be the change in her circumstances.

He could not believe that a titled brother and a dowry of £20,000 would change Sarah, but what other explanation could there be? His warm, honest, open Sarah had turned into a cold, hard and cynical young woman . . . He straightened up and looked round the room, making sure he had not forgotten anything; he had left for Bath in such a hurry that he had not brought his valet and was doing all his packing himself. He had just satisfied himself that nothing of his remained when there came a knock at the door. He called out curtly, 'Come.'

The door opened to reveal one of the boys who ran errands around the inn.

'Well?' demanded James, in no mood to be civil.

'Are you Lord Randall?' the boy asked.

'Of course I am,' said James impatiently.

'There's a footman downstairs, come with a message for you. From a Miss Davenport.'

James's mouth set in a grim line: the last

thing he wanted was a letter from Sarah. 'Tell him to leave it with the landlord. I will collect it when I come down.'

'Says it's urgent,' offered the boy.

'When I come down,' repeated James severely.

The boy wavered, and then deciding he was more in awe of the tall gentleman before him than he was of the landlord, he returned to his master below.

James closed his travelling bag, trying hard to keep his mind from the note. Whatever it said, he did not want to read it. But he was curious all the same.

He picked up his bag and went downstairs.

'And don't forget your letter, my lord,' said the landlord ingratiatingly as James settled his account and was about to leave.

It was the last thing James wanted. He had no desire to read a letter from Sarah, but he took it anyway. He wrestled with himself but at last his curiosity got the better of him and he opened the note.

My darling James, he read.

His black brows shot up in surprise. Was it some sort of forgery?

He looked closely at the writing, but no, it was not forged: the writing was definitely Sarah's.

As he read the rest of the note his surprise gave way to perplexity. The message was extraordinary. It was such gibberish that he wondered if she could have been ill—feverish—when she wrote it. Despite himself he felt concerned.

'When did this message arrive?' he asked the landlord.

'Just a few minutes ago, my lord. The footman who brought it is in the tap-room waiting to see if there's a reply.'

James folded up the letter and went into the tap-room, where the footman came forward immediately.

'Did you bring this letter?' demanded James.

'Yes, my lord.'

'And who gave it to you?'

'The butler, my lord: Miss Davenport told him it was to be delivered straight away.'

'And how did she seem when she spoke to him?' asked James. 'Did she seem ill in any way?'

'No, my lord,' said the footman in surprise. 'She was just about to go out with the gentleman.'

'Her brother?' asked James.

'Oh, no, my lord. The other gentleman. The one from Watermead Grange.'

A cold feeling invaded the pit of James's stomach. Why would anyone be visiting Sarah from the Grange? Unless . . .

'Describe him.'

'Fair, my lord, and of slight build. No more than two or three inches taller than Miss

Davenport, I should say.'

'Haversage,' ground out James between clenched teeth.

The footman looked startled.

When he next spoke, James's face was grim. 'I need to speak to the butler. Right away.'

* * *

'So this is it,' said Sarah as she stepped out of the hired carriage and looked at the shack in front of her. 'This is your "cottage".'

'It may not look much to you,' said Mr Haversage with an unsettling hint of manic laughter in his voice, 'but it's home.'

'And where is Lucy?' demanded Sarah. 'Take me to her at once.'

'As you wish,' said Mr Haversage. 'Lucy is just inside.'

Sarah had the uncomfortable feeling that it was a trap. But with Lucy's safety at stake she could not refuse to go in. Steeling herself for what she might find, she preceded Mr Haversage into the derelict building.

The room she walked into was small and damp. A flight of stone steps led upwards at the back of the room.

'Lucy!' called Sarah. 'Lucy, don't be afraid.'

'How very touching,' Mr Haversage mocked. 'But there's no need to shout, Sarah. You can talk to Lucy all you want. As long as I get the money, you can have her back safe and sound.'

Sarah went to the back of the room and, lifting the hem of her skirt so that she would not trip, she climbed the uneven stairs. The room above was as damp and miserable as the room below, but there was no sign of Lucy. Instead, Maud de Bracy was there.

'Mrs de Bracy!' gasped Sarah. 'Has he demanded money from you, too?'

Her first thought was that Mr Haversage was using Lucy to gain money from a number of sources, but as soon as Maud laughed she knew that she was wrong.

'Where's Lucy?' she demanded, rounding on Mr Haversage.

'Lucy's back at Watermead Grange.'

'But the hair . . .?'

And then, suddenly, Sarah had a flash of memory, a flash of finding Nelly in her room.

Things began to fall into place.

'You got Nelly to cut her hair. It was Nelly who gave it to you, wasn't it? Neatly tied with the pink ribbon Lucy wore at the concert?'

He smiled, but the smile did not reach his eyes. 'Nelly has been very useful, one way or another.'

'You set her to spy on me,' said Sarah accusingly.

'You, and everyone else in the Grange. Knowledge is power, Sarah. One never knows when it will come in useful. Your brother's address in Bath was certainly worth knowing—

Nelly found it on one of the letters he had sent to you. It's such a pity you discovered her in your room. Her snooping sessions had to come to an end.'

'But why the charade?' demanded Sarah, wanting to know the extent of Mr Haversage's plan. 'You must have known I wouldn't hand over the money without seeing Lucy first.'

'Do you still not see it?' laughed Mr Haversage. 'This has never been about Lucy. This has all been about you. Why should I go to all the risk of kidnapping Lucy from the Grange, where she is surrounded by servants day and night, when I can get you to walk into my trap of your own accord?'

'Nicholas will never pay,' said Sarah stoutly.

'Nicholas will never have to,' said Maud dryly. Up until now she had been content to let Mr Haversage do the talking, but now she wanted to take her part. 'It's James who will pay. Pay for slighting me—'

'And pay for criticizing me,' interrupted Mr Haversage. 'Me!' His voice was growing dangerous. 'Telling *me* what to do and what not to do, like the arrogant, conceited bastard he is.'

'You surely can't expect Lord Randall to ransom me?' asked Sarah in astonishment.

'*Lord Randall*? You can drop the pretence. *My darling James.* That's what he is to you.'

And Sarah laughed. She knew she was in danger but the tension that had gripped her since Mr Haversage had walked into Laura Place needed some release, and it came in the form of slightly hysterical laughter.

'What's so funny?' asked Mr Haversage.

'Ignore her,' snapped Maud. 'Can't you see she's only playing for time? Now do what we brought her here for, and then we can contact James.'

'She means something by it,' said Mr Haversage suspiciously.

'She means nothing! Now get on with it,' said Maud. 'Here, I'll hold her down for you and you can finish what you started at the ruins.' She gave an ugly smile. 'I'd like to see the look on James's face when he realizes the goods he's ransomed are soiled.'

She moved towards Sarah, and Sarah, once more in control of herself, backed away. Now she knew why she had been lured here: so that Mr Haversage could rape her. And so that, afterwards, she could be used to get money from James. But she was not going to let that happen. She could not overpower both Mr Haversage and Mrs de Bracy, so she would have to use her brains instead.

'You may well get a chance to do that, Maud,' Sarah said. 'James is on his way here at this moment.'

'Don't be ridiculous,' said Maud with contempt. 'He knows nothing about it.'

'The message!' spat Mr Haversage.

'What message?' demanded Maud. Now it

was her turn to round on him.

'There *was* no meeting,' said Sarah. 'No soirée, no affair. James and I parted on the worst possible terms. As soon as he reads the letter he'll know something's wrong. How long do you think it will take him after that to find out where I've gone?'

'The carriage,' said Mr Haversage to Maud. 'The driver will tell him where we are. I knew we should never have hired one. If you hadn't been such a skinflint we could have bought one.'

'What with?' she scoffed.

Whilst they were arguing, Sarah worked out the rudiments of a plan. If she could get them to take her elsewhere, then she would have a chance to escape. Once out of this small room, where both Maud and Mr Haversage were standing between her and the stairs, she would have room to run or fight. But they would not take her out of the room if she asked them to do so. She would have to pretend she wanted to stay.

'So all *I* have to do,' she said, with a calmness she was far from feeling, 'is sit and wait.'

She suited her actions to her words, sitting on a rickety chair. It almost gave way beneath her as she did so.

'Oh, no, you don't,' said Maud. She grabbed Sarah's arm. 'When James gets here, he'll find nothing but an empty hovel.'

Outside, though, James had already arrived.

It had not taken him long to locate the hired carriage that had carried Sarah and Mr Haversage to the cottage, and the driver—for a handsome fee—had driven James there, leaving him a short distance away so that the carriage should be neither seen nor heard.

As James assessed the situation, knowing that Sarah was somewhere inside but that rash action could endanger her life, he heard a commotion and saw a figure coming out of the door. It was Mr Haversage. Behind him came Sarah, and then . . . Maud de Bracy.

His mouth set in a grim line. Maud. He had not suspected her jealousy would carry her this far: not only to financing Mr Haversage, but to taking an active part in Sarah's abduction. She was holding Sarah by the arm now, forcing her along behind Mr Haversage—but Sarah, turning suddenly and catching Maud off balance, broke free.

James was upon them in an instant. He leapt across the intervening scrubland, catching Mr Haversage's arm just as he was preparing to bring it down on Sarah's head.

'Not this time, Haversage; not ever,' he said, his muscles like steel as they bore Mr Haversage's arm further and further back.

'Randall!' said Mr Haversage, his face going white. It was one thing to attack a woman; quite another to face a hardened man.

'James!' cried Sarah. And despite her

predicament her heart soared.

It was the only chance Maud needed. With Sarah momentarily distracted, and James twisting Mr Haversage's arm behind his back into an unbreakable lock, she whipped a small pistol out of her reticule.

'Let him go,' she said.

James looked at her unflinchingly. 'No.'

'Let him go, I say.'

'You don't care enough about Haversage to kill for him,' said James commandingly. 'Put the gun away.'

'Haversage is nothing,' she said. 'Nevertheless, you are going to let both him and me walk away. No one is going to ruin my reputation, James; neither him nor you.'

'Your reputation's ruined already,' said James. He held out his free hand, whilst putting pressure on Mr Haversage's arm with the other to keep him compliant. 'Give me the gun.'

'If I walk away from this with Haversage, then no one will ever know what happened here,' said Maud, waving the gun at him more purposefully. 'But if I let you take Haversage he will drag me down with him at his trial. He will tell everyone that I helped him abduct the little bitch. And I'm not about to let that happen. I have too much to lose. So you are going to let him go.'

'I can't do that,' said James steadfastly.

'Oh, no?' enquired Maud. She turned the

gun until it was pointing at Sarah. 'Can you do it now?'

James wavered. Maud saw it and smiled. Sarah, taking advantage of Maud's momentary lapse of concentration, acted more quickly than thought, and in a single fluid movement knocked Maud's arm sideways. Shocked, Maud pulled the trigger in a reflex action, just as Mr Haversage, making the most of the confusion, broke away from James. There was a loud report, and then Mr Haversage, with a startled expression on his face, fell to his knees.

Time seemed to stand still. Mr Haversage, clutching at his chest, remained on his knees for a minute, and then fell forwards with a dull thud.

* * *

How Sarah got through the next few hours she did not know. Despite her strong character she felt light-headed as she did what she could to staunch Mr Haversage's wound. He had not been killed by the shot, and she made every effort to keep him alive whilst James saw to Maud. Unhinged by the accident—for she had never meant to shoot anyone, and had only meant to frighten James into letting her go so that her reputation would not be ruined by her involvement in the scandalous affair—Maud had become hysterical, and James had had to act quickly in order to prevent her from taking her own life.

Events after that had moved rapidly. The coach-driver who had taken James to the cottage had returned when he heard the shot, and had been sent by James to fetch the authorities. There were questions and explanations, but fortunately James's father had been well known in Bath and the matter was therefore conducted with a great deal of discretion.

Sarah, as soon as she was no longer needed, and worn out by the events of the morning, retreated to a fallen tree and sat down, grateful for a few minutes' peace and quiet in which to relax her overstretched nerves.

James, excusing himself, went over to her. Looking down at her he was filled with feelings of longing and tenderness. Their argument seemed unimportant in the face of everything that had happened since.

'Sarah . . . Sarah . . .' he said, sitting down beside her. Her hair had come loose of its pins and a gleaming auburn strand fell across her white face. He reached out his hand and stroked it back behind her ear. His fingers lingered, savouring the contact with the beautiful young woman before him. Because even now, to him, she was beautiful, though her face was white and her features drawn.

'Sarah, I thought I'd lost you.'

She turned towards him. His eyes were

every bit as black and velvety as she remembered, and they were full of tenderness and concern.

'Would it have mattered? If you had?'

'You can ask that?'

'I didn't know . . .'

'This has all been a terrible ordeal for you,' he said, seeing how drawn she looked. He took her hands. They were icy. Gently he began to chafe them. 'I should have brought a hip-flask,' he said. 'Some brandy is just what you need to warm you through.'

Sarah gave a wry smile. 'I'm glad you didn't. Once was enough. Besides,' she added, her smile softening as she looked down at his hands, which were massaging her own, 'I think I prefer this way of warming through.'

He smiled; a warm smile. Just for a moment it was as though they were back in the picture gallery at Watermead Grange, with no arguments and misunderstandings standing between them.

Her hair fell loose again and he pushed it back, this time pinning it so that it would stay in place. The feel of his fingers on her scalp was soothing, and she wondered briefly how it was that his hands, which had produced such electric sensations within her on her last night at the Grange, could now be so comforting.

'James—'

'There will be time for explanations later. For now, I'm just glad that you are safe. It took courage to tackle Maud like that,' he said.

Sarah gave a rueful smile.

'I don't think it was courage. I think it was more like desperation. I couldn't let her pull the trigger—at least not without trying to stop her.' She frowned. 'I never realized that Maud was so unhinged.'

'Nor did I. If I'd known I'd never have let her anywhere near you.'

'You weren't to blame.'

She shivered, remembering Maud's unbalanced behaviour.

'Here,' he said. He took off his coat, revealing his snowy linen and the outlines of his powerful chest. He put the coat round her shoulders.

Sarah snuggled into it. It was warm and musky, and carried the lingering scent of him.

'You look exhausted,' he said. 'This has all been too much for you. You shouldn't still be here.' He turned and beckoned the coachman. 'I'm sending you back to Laura Place.'

'Are you not . . .?' she asked, disappointed that he did not mean to go with her. The look on his face when Maud had levelled the gun at her had given her hope that James's feelings for her were as deep and sincere as her feelings for him, and their earlier misunderstandings, at that moment, seemed no more than a bad dream.

'I can't come yet,' he said regretfully. 'There are still a number of formalities to be attended to. But I don't want you here whilst they're dealt with. There's no need for you to be involved in this any more than you have been. I will come and see you as soon as possible. In the meantime,' he said, helping her to her feet and leading her over to the coach, 'you need to get some rest.'

For once, Sarah had no desire to argue, and was relieved when James handed her into the coach, giving the coachman instructions to see her safely back to Laura Place.

The journey was not a long one, and Sarah was pleased to find herself once more among familiar surroundings. On her return she had to give a brief account of the affair to her worried brothers but then she was free to retire to her room. Her nerves had been strained to the limit, and she was glad to have a chance to rest before James arrived.

* * *

'I don't like it, Nick,' said Geoffrey, as the two brothers sat in the library talking over Sarah's ordeal.

'Neither do I.'

'How could Randall let Sarah get mixed up in something like that?'

Sarah's account of her ordeal had been sketchy and, as she had been suffering the after-effects of shock, not very coherent. So that Nicholas and Geoffrey had formed no very accurate idea of what had happened. The one thing they *had* been able to make out was that Sarah had been involved in a dangerous and frightening situation, and that Lord Randall had somehow been involved.

'The man's a scoundrel,' said Nicholas shortly.

He had never met Lord Randall, but Sarah's early letters from the Grange in which she had painted James as a cold-hearted and arrogant monster, together with this latest situation, had been enough to convince him that Lord Randall was a dreadful man.

'Why did he have to come to Bath in the first place?' complained Geoffrey. 'He's no business here. He should have stayed in Kent.'

'I wish he had,' said Nicholas. 'It would have saved a lot of trouble, and a lot of distress. But as he hasn't it's up to me, as the head of the family, to make sure he doesn't bother Sarah again.' He was taking his new responsibilities seriously, and was determined to protect his sister, whatever the cost.

'Yes, but what can you do?' asked Geoffrey practically.

'I can spare her any more of Randall's attentions,' said Nicholas. 'Starting today. If he tries to see Sarah I've given strict instructions he must be told that Miss Davenport is not at home. I won't have him bothering her, or leading her into difficult or dangerous situations.'

‘Good for you, Nick. Show him you mean business. But what if he calls again tomorrow?’

‘The answer will still be the same. And the day after that and the day after that: Miss Davenport is not at home.’

CHAPTER THIRTEEN

Lady Templeton was reclining on an elegant *chaise-longue* in the sitting-room of her London home. On the chair facing her sat a middle-aged woman, her new companion, who was reading aloud from *Pride and Prejudice*, one of Lady Templeton’s favourite books. But despite Griselda’s lively reading, Lady Templeton could not keep her mind on the story, entertaining though it was.

‘Thank you, Griselda,’ she said as her companion reached the end of a page, ‘but I think I have heard enough for now.’

Griselda looked at her enquiringly. Lady Templeton usually liked to hear a chapter at a time, and she wondered if anything was wrong.

‘No, nothing,’ said Lady Templeton, in answer to her question. Saying a minute later, ‘Oh, what’s the use of denying it. Yes, there is something wrong. It’s this estrangement between Sarah and James.’

She had seen her nephew on his return from Bath and, although James had meant to say nothing about it, she had learnt the full story. It had not surprised her. James and Sarah had seemed so eminently suited that she had been half expecting them to fall in love for months.

'Who would have thought it,' said Griselda sympathetically, 'Miss Davenport thinking he was only proposing to her because she was no longer a governess?'

'I would. In her own way, Sarah is just as proud as James. Her pride never spills over into arrogance, but nevertheless she has a healthy amount of self-respect. And what young lady with any self-respect would accept a man who made no attempt to tell her that he loved her when she was a penniless governess, but declared his feelings as soon as her situation changed?'

'But it wasn't like that!' protested Griselda.

'I know that, and you know that, Griselda, but Sarah doesn't. And now, with Sarah constantly saying she is "not at home", there is no way for her ever to learn her mistake.'

'You don't agree with Lord Randall, then, that if she loved him she would trust him? You don't think that, if she truly loved him, she would know that he could never propose to her just because of her changed circumstances?'

'But she *does* trust him,' said Lady Templeton. 'Why else would she have turned to him when that wretched tutor abducted her? She had her brothers to turn to. Why, then, turn to James, if she did not trust him?'

Griselda sighed in agreement. Her tender heart felt for the young couple, and she indulged herself in a momentary wish that she could wave a magic wand and set everything to rights. Magic wands being in short supply at Templeton House, however, she had to content herself with paying attention to Lady Templeton instead!

'Even James recognized it,' she said. 'He knew it himself. Which is why he went to see Sarah, after he had seen to all the formalities; to set everything between them to rights.'

'And that is when she refused to see him?'

Lady Templeton sighed. 'That, and every other time he called. She was never "at home".'

The two ladies were silent for a time. And then, 'It doesn't make sense!' declared Lady Templeton. 'Why wouldn't she see him? It isn't like Sarah to hide herself away. She is an honest, open person; forthright and outspoken. Something must be behind it. And I mean to find out what.'

'But what can you do?' asked Griselda with a sigh.

'I can bring them face to face,' said Lady Templeton practically. 'And if they don't end up reconciled at the end of their meeting, then I will wash my hands of them altogether!'

Griselda shook her head sorrowfully. 'It would be nice if you could do it. But how?'

'As to that,' said Lady Templeton with a

twinkle in her eye, 'I have an idea.'

* * *

The days passed slowly for Sarah.

At first she had expected James to call at any moment, but as the hours had dragged by, turning into days and then into weeks she had had to accept at last that he did not mean to come.

She had been so sure, at the moment when Maud had levelled the pistol at her, that James loved her. The fear in his eyes—fear which had been wholly absent when the gun was pointing at himself—had told her far more eloquently than words could ever have done, just how much she meant to him. And his conduct towards her following the ordeal had been tender and concerned. But why, then, did he not come? Especially as he had told her that, as soon as the formalities had been attended to, he would call on her straight away.

Small consolation now for her to tell herself that, if he had made so little effort to mend matters between them, then he was not worthy of her love. For she was in no doubt about her feelings for him now. She was in love with him. And it was useless to pretend otherwise.

'Not by the window again, Sarah?' asked Nicholas, strolling into the drawing-room.

Sarah started. She had been so lost in her

thoughts she had not heard him come in.

She was about to ask him what he meant by his comment when she changed her mind. She often sat by the window, and she knew it was because, deep down, no matter how foolish it might be, she still hoped that James would come.

'Are you going to the Pump Room this afternoon?' he asked her.

'No.' She shook her head.

'You should do. You look pale.' Nicholas shuffled his feet. He wondered, not for the first time, if he might have been wrong in ordering the servants to say that Miss Davenport was 'not at home'; and he also wondered if he had been wrong to keep the knowledge of Lord Randall's repeated calls from Sarah herself. But then he told himself that it was all for the best. Sarah would eventually get over it—although why she should be pining over such an arrogant monster was beyond Nicholas's twenty-one-year-old understanding—and she was much better off without a man who had involved her in a scandalous and dangerous situation.

His reflections were interrupted by Aunt Claire entering the room with the post.

'A letter for you, Nicholas,' she said, handing him a perfumed letter. 'And one for you, Sarah. And the rest are for me,' she said with a self-satisfied air, before retiring to her room to read her letters.

Sarah took her letter eagerly, but to her dismay she saw that it was not from James. It was instead, judging by the handwriting, from Lady Templeton.

The two of them had exchanged letters about the children, and Sarah had been pleased to learn that Nelly had been dismissed from the Grange for her part in Mr Haversage's plans. As Sarah read through Lady Templeton's latest letter she was interested to discover that her ladyship thought she had found a suitable governess for Lucy. *But I would value your opinion, Sarah*, the letter went on, before suggesting that Sarah should pay a visit to Templeton House where she could meet the young lady in question.

'You won't go, of course,' said Nicholas, when Sarah had told him the contents of the letter.

'Of course I will,' said Sarah. She still thought about the children, and until she knew they had a kind and loving governess to look after them she would feel badly about having left them so suddenly.

'Sarah, this isn't wise,' said Nicholas with a frown.

'Why ever not?' asked Sarah in surprise.

'You have done with that family,' he said. There was a hint of anger in his voice; anger directed at himself rather than Sarah, because despite his belief that he had acted in her best interests he was not by nature deceitful, and he did not like to think that he had done anything underhand. 'After the way they have treated you, I wonder at you wanting to have anything more to do with them.'

'What *do* you mean?' asked Sarah in surprise.

'Only this,' remarked Nicholas. 'That you have had nothing but unhappiness from that family. They have treated you with nothing but disdain. And, as head of the household, I cannot allow you to go.'

'You can't stop me,' said Sarah with a note of finality in her voice. 'I left Watermead Grange without giving any notice, and I feel myself honour bound to do what I can to help find a suitable replacement to look after the children. I'm very fond of them, Nick. They're dear children, and I don't want them to suffer just because the fortunes of their ex-governess have changed. Until I know they're in the charge of a good, sensible woman, I won't be happy.'

'In that case, you had better go.' Nicholas's voice was unusually grudging. 'I only hope you don't live to regret it.'

Sarah was again surprised. 'Why should I regret it?'

'Come on, Sarah.' Nicholas fell back into their childhood speech. 'Because Lady Templeton is Lord Randall's aunt.'

'And you're afraid I may run across him?

You can set your mind at ease on that score. If Lord Randall had wanted to see me he would have come to Laura Place by now. But he hasn't. And once he knows I am to visit his aunt, he will certainly stay away.'

Nicholas could say no more. His one hope was that Lord Randall would not learn of Sarah's visit to London until it was too late; until Sarah was safely back in Bath.

* * *

'Miss Susannah Grey is a sensible young woman,' said Lady Templeton the following week, as she and Sarah took tea together in the drawing-room of Templeton House. 'She is the cousin of Sir Richard Petheroe, and is at present a member of his household.'

'Do you think she would accept the post?' asked Sarah. As she looked around her she thought how many things had changed since she had last visited the house. Little had she known at the time just how different her life would become.

'I think she might. Sir Richard is kind enough in his way, but Susannah has no real purpose in his household. She is, however, of an energetic nature and I think she would like to have something definite to do. Her principles are good, and although she doesn't have your strength of character she is good-tempered and kind. But you will soon see her for yourself. I have invited the Petheroes to dine, and they are to bring Susannah with them.'

They heard the sound of a carriage drawing up outside.

'Ah! Here they are now,' said Lady Templeton.

The Petheroes were soon admitted. Their party consisted of Sir Richard and his wife, their two elder sons, and Susannah. Susannah, Sarah was pleased to see, looked a good sort of girl. She was rather young, being only eighteen, but Sarah was not worried about her standing up to James, because she no longer felt that standing up to him was necessary, at least as far as the children were concerned. His views—under her influence—had changed so drastically that she was confident he would let them be children: he had adjusted wonderfully to their needs, and to the more relaxed nature of civilian life.

After a little conversation with Susannah she found that there was nothing to object to in the girl. Although she felt a pang at the thought of no longer being Lucy's governess she was too generous to give in to it. She was determined that Lucy should not suffer by her absence, and Susannah was undoubtedly a suitable replacement. Susannah had a good heart and good principles. She was very accomplished and, more important, she had a warm and affectionate nature. She would teach Lucy well, Sarah was sure, and would encourage her, rather than repressing her. All in all, Sarah felt Lady Templeton had done well to find such a suitable young lady.

They were just about to go into dinner when the double doors into the drawing-room opened again, and the butler announced, 'Lord Randall, my lady.'

Sarah felt the blood rush to her cheeks. James? Here? Tonight?

It took all of her strength of will to recover at least some of her composure. She had been confident that she would not see him at Lady Templeton's house; if she had been any less confident she would not have come. He had made it quite clear what he thought of her by his absence from Laura Place, and to be forced to meet him here, at his aunt's house, and over dinner too, was one of the worst moments of her life.

He felt it, too. He checked immediately on seeing her, and if she had had any doubts about his hostility towards her his expression would have dispelled them. A cold, haughty mask spread almost instantly over his face.

'Ah! James! There you are!' said Lady Templeton with forced ease.

For she had to admit, if only to herself, that the hostility which had suddenly filled the room did not bode well.

'Randall! Good to see you!' said Sir Richard. Fortunately he knew nothing of what was going on, and was therefore able to behave normally. 'And how are you liking life now you're out of the army? Glad all the fighting's over, eh? Must have been very satisfying, putting paid to old Boney at last. Peace took a long time coming, but it was worth it. Who knows? Now that King Louis is in charge again, I might even be brave enough to take a trip to France!'

James replied politely and, once the party had made their way into the dining-room, continued talking to Sir Richard. The two gentlemen talked on a wide variety of topics, ranging from the refurbishment of the Marine Pavilion at Brighton to the price of grain. But whatever the subject under discussion, James's eyes kept drifting to Sarah. She was looking pale, he thought, and, contrary to what he had expected, she did not appear to be happy.

Sarah herself could not but help be aware of James's attention, and no matter how hard she tried to focus on her conversation with Susannah she kept wondering what his constant looks might mean. If he despised her as much as she supposed he must, then why was he looking at her at all?

'. . . for the ladies to withdraw.'

Sarah had been so lost in her thoughts that she almost missed Lady Templeton's pronouncement, but she caught it just in time and the ladies withdrew, leaving the gentlemen to their port.

* * *

'What do you think, Sarah?' asked Lady Templeton, as Susannah occupied herself by looking through a book of sketches at the far side of the drawing-room.

'I think she would be very suitable,' said Sarah. 'She seems very agreeable. Has she any experience of children?'

'She has a younger sister and brother, so she is used to children and their ways.'

'Yes, I think she would be an excellent choice,' said Sarah.

'Good, good,' said Lady Templeton. 'Then we are agreed. Tomorrow I will speak to James.'

'You didn't mention that Lord Randall was going to be here tonight,' said Sarah with an air of apparent unconcern.

'I thought it as well to invite him. It is his niece we are trying to help, after all.' Although not the whole truth Lady Templeton was convinced—more particularly so after seeing the way James had been unable to keep his eyes off Sarah at dinner—that her small deception was all in a good cause.

'Of course,' replied Sarah. She tried to make her voice light and unconcerned.

The gentlemen did not linger over their port and soon returned to the ladies, whereupon Lady Templeton set up a card-table as she knew that Sir Richard and his two sons always liked to play. Susannah joined them and Lady Templeton, by a little adroit management, drew Sir Richard's wife into conversation, leaving Sarah and James as the only two people who were not otherwise engaged.

To cover the awkwardness of the situation, Sarah pretended to be interested in the book of sketches that had so recently occupied Susannah, and James, after fighting a short battle with himself, followed her to the far side of the room.

He watched her in silence for a minute or two, minutes which to Sarah seemed to stretch into eternity, before saying at last, 'You have always been honest with me, Sarah, so answer me just one question: why did you refuse to see me in Bath?'

Sarah was so surprised at this question that for a minute she could not reply. Was it some kind of ruse? Some attempt to put the blame on her?

'Do you still believe I had an ulterior motive in offering you my hand?'

She shook her head. 'Not an ulterior motive. But . . .'

'Yes?'

'But if I had still been a governess . . .'

'You think I would have said nothing? You think I would have left you to go your way? And you think I would have gone mine?'

Sarah sighed. 'You are a very proud man, James. You wouldn't let Dominic marry Miss Yardley, and her position is far higher than mine was until a few weeks ago. Why should I think that, after telling Dominic he couldn't marry an eligible young lady simply because she was not his equal in rank that you, as an earl, would stoop so low as to marry a governess?'

'So that's the reason.' There was an unmistakable sound of satisfaction in James's voice, coupled with a note of relief. She hadn't changed. She hadn't been spoiled by her good fortune. She was still his Sarah. He knew now that her reaction to his proposal had been justified, and he smiled a wry smile. 'That's why you doubted me. Because I wouldn't let Dom marry Miss Yardley.'

'I know your views on unequal marriages too well,' she said, determined to make him understand why she had been so angry. 'If you'd loved me, then perhaps—'

'Do you doubt it?' he asked.

'In the woods that night . . .' she began, fighting down an impossible hope.

'It was a terrible mistake. Sarah, I'm sorry—'

'That's just it. You're sorry. I'm not. I know I should be ashamed to admit it, but I'm not sorry at all.'

'Really?' He gave her a wicked smile.

'Don't look at me like that,' she said, uncomfortably aware that his closeness was having a profound effect on her. 'It isn't fair. It was obvious you regretted—'

'Almost seducing you? Yes, I did. It was unforgivable. No gentleman would ever seduce his niece's governess, no matter what his feelings might be.'

'So that's why you were horrified?' She could not hide the delight in her voice.

'Yes,' he said, taking her hand and stroking it. 'That's why I was horrified. I didn't regret what we'd shared; not for a minute. But I was horrified to realize I'd nearly taken advantage of you.'

Sarah was finding it difficult to concentrate. Nevertheless, she went on. 'But that still doesn't alter the fact that you told Dominic he would never be happy if he married beneath him.'

'I don't deny it.' There was a strange look—almost a gleam of humour—in James's eye, but Sarah could not for the life of her think of its cause. 'He wouldn't have been happy. Miss Yardley is a very vulgar young woman.'

'Dominic didn't think so,' remarked Sarah, thinking: and neither did Mrs Smith. Not knowing that the good Mrs Smith had never met her.

James looked at her curiously, stopping his stroking for the moment. 'Do you really believe I talked Dom out of offering for Miss Yardley simply because she wasn't his equal in rank?'

Sarah sighed. 'If outspokenness is my besetting sin, then pride is most definitely yours.'

James smiled. This was the open and honest person he had fallen in love with. And she had a point. But she did not know the whole story.

'You don't think she might really be vulgar?' he asked. 'You don't think she might really be beneath Dominic, not because she is not his equal in rank, but because her character is flawed as well?'

Sarah did not answer. She clearly thought that that would not be the case.

'What if I was to give you the opportunity of finding out? Miss Yardley is in London. Nothing would be easier than for me to invite her to Randall House.'

Now that he knew the cause of Sarah's fears, he was determined to lay them to rest.

'And if she isn't vulgar?' asked Sarah. 'If her character isn't flawed? What happens then?'

'If you think Dom would be happy with her, then I'll withdraw all my objections to the match. I'll even stand up with Dom at his wedding.'

'And you will really be guided by me?'

'Haven't I been guided by you before? When you told me the children needed to play, didn't I listen to you? When you told me Lucy and Preston should join us at the boating-party didn't I see your point of view? When you told me I must let the children arrange a concert, didn't I agree?'

'Eventually,' she conceded. She could not resist a smile.

James's mouth gave an answering quirk. 'Well, Sarah? Do you accept my challenge?'

Sarah did not hesitate. 'I do.'

'I do,' he repeated. 'I like the sound of that.'

Sarah felt a tingle run down her spine.

He could not resist it. He leant forward and kissed her on her soft, fragrant cheek. 'Then it's agreed?'

'Agreed. And I look forward to hearing wedding-bells,' she said significantly, thinking how happy Dominic would be when James at last gave his blessing to the match.

James gave her a meaningful look. 'So do I, Sarah.'

And, as Sarah stood up and went over to join the two ladies on the sofa, he said again under his breath, 'So do I.'

CHAPTER FOURTEEN

'I must say, I think this is an excellent idea,' said Lady Templeton a few days later as she and Sarah, accompanied by Griselda, were admitted to Randall House. 'I have been longing to see the new drawing-room. It was such a wreck in James's father's time. Hannibal was a dear man, but he had absolutely no taste. Now with James in charge, I expect to see a vast improvement.'

James had wasted no time in sending out invitations. Lady Templeton had been delighted. Sarah, too, had been pleased. The listlessness that had assailed her in Bath had vanished and she was looking forward to meeting the elusive Miss Yardley. And, even more, she was looking forward to proving James wrong. Little knowing that James, too, was looking forward to the afternoon, because he was looking forward to punishing Sarah, ever so gently, for having doubted his motives for proposing to her.

'Miss Yardley isn't here, then?' asked Sarah, as James welcomed her into his splendid London home.

'Not yet. But you are early,' said James. 'I'm sure she'll be on time.'

Their voices were low. Of all those at Randall House that afternoon, only the two of them knew why the tea-party had been arranged, and why Miss Yardley had been invited.

'But it's splendid, James. Simply splendid.' Lady Templeton looked appreciatively round the beautifully refurbished room.

'It is. It's lovely,' said Sarah. The drawing-room was painted in warm shades of cream, with a beautifully painted green-and-cream ceiling. The white marble fireplace, with a large mirror above it, brightened the room whilst the inlaid console tables and low gilded chairs gave a restrained air of grandeur.

'The final touches need adding,' said James. He turned to Sarah. 'I was hoping you might have some ideas.'

Sarah felt a warm glow of happiness as he asked for her opinion. 'I think the Sèvres vase would be better on the console table,' she said. 'It's overshadowed by the landscape at present. And a bowl of flowers would look lovely on the escritoire.'

His eyes twinkled. 'It shall be just as you say.'

Sarah laughed. 'It seems I am now giving you orders, my lord,' she teased him.

'Who better?' he smiled in return.

Hearing their banter Lady Templeton caught Griselda's eye, and both ladies smiled. So far, the day was going very well!

Sarah spent a very pleasant ten minutes discussing the colour of new carpets and curtains with James, before Lady Templeton brought their attention back to the present by remarking, 'Miss Yardley seems to be rather late.'

'So she is.' Sarah looked at James, but instead of looking concerned he looked, if anything, pleased. Sarah began to find her confidence in the unknown young lady slipping away. Could she be mistaken in her ideas about Miss Yardley? Was it possible that Miss Yardley might be a truly vulgar young woman who would appear in a transparent gown and with a heavily rouged face?

But she need not have worried. Miss Yardley, when she at last arrived with her father some half an hour late, was a lovely young lady. She was demurely dressed in a beautiful sky-blue day-dress, trimmed with fringing in a darker blue. The waist of the gown was high, as was the neckline, which revealed nothing it should not reveal, and it was finished off with a white ruff.

All in all, as Sarah looked at her, she was well pleased.

Miss Yardley's first words impressed her still further. In a melodious voice Miss Yardley apologized for her late arrival.

Good manners as well as beauty, thought Sarah. Dominic has chosen well.

She glanced at James, expecting him to look chagrined, but he looked no such thing. Instead there was a hint of a smile lurking at the corner of his mouth.

Ah! It is to be a battle of wills, thought Sarah. So be it! Let it begin!

'We set out in good time,' explained Miss Yardley, as the footman came in with a tray of china cups and saucers, and a large silver teapot. 'Such good time, that we just had time to call in at the draper's—Grafton House, I expect you know it—on the way. Didn't we, Pa?'

'Aye lass, that we did.'

Miss Yardley's 'Pa' was a bluff Lancastrian. He had a red face and a portly figure, which had been squeezed into white silk knee-breeches, a patterned waistcoat, and an old-fashioned, full-skirted coat reminiscent of those worn in his youth. But despite his expensive clothes, Mr Yardley remained what he was: a bluff, self-made man, who verged on being uncouth.

Sarah could see at once why James objected to him. Without polish or education, he was clearly out of place in the elegant drawing-room. As she watched him pour his tea into his saucer and blow on it noisily, Sarah thought she could see why James objected so strongly to Miss Yardley becoming Dominic's wife.

But Miss Yardley was not responsible for her father's failings, and although Sarah had to admit to herself that the loud slurping noise coming from Mr Yardley's direction as he drank his tea was rather off-putting, she was determined that Miss Yardley should not be punished for having such a—she searched her mind for a kindly description—for such a *colourful* father.

'And would you believe it?' Miss Yardley went on, sipping delicately at her own tea. 'They were just unpacking the best assortment of silks and satins you ever did see. So of course I said to Pa, "I just can't afford to miss this opportunity". Didn't I, Pa?' She went on straight away, without giving her father time to put down his saucer and reply. 'There was a rose-pink satin I just had to have, wasn't there, Pa?'

Sarah's smile, which had become somewhat fixed, began to fade. That Miss Yardley should have been delayed was unfortunate, but it seemed that she had not been delayed at all. Instead she had delayed herself, and had caused considerable inconvenience to her host by refusing to put off her shopping trip.

'And do you know,' went on Miss Yardley, 'that adorable satin was only eighteen shillings a yard. Wasn't it, Pa?'

'Aye, lass, that it was.'

'And a darling spotted muslin, only eight shillings a yard. And a primrose silk, though that was more than a pound a yard. Still, as I said to Pa, "A ball gown's not a ball gown unless it's over a pound a yard." Didn't I, Pa?'

'Aye, lass. You did,' said her father ponderously, looking at his startled audience with satisfaction.

That they were startled at his daughter's vulgar catalogue of prices he did not realize. He thought they were startled and impressed over the amount of money he and his daughter had to spend.

'Your gown is silk, is it not?' said Miss Yardley shrewdly to Lady Templeton. 'And a very fine silk, too. It must have cost all of—no, don't tell me,' she said, putting out her hand as if to forestall Lady Templeton.

'I wouldn't dream of it,' remarked Lady Templeton dryly.

But her dryness was lost on Miss Yardley.

'It must have cost all of . . . I should say it must have cost all of thirty shillings a yard,' went on that indefatigable young woman.

At this point, Sarah caught sight of James out of the corner of her eye. The smile which had lurked at the corner of his mouth ever since he had suggested she should meet Miss Yardley was threatening to become a smirk!' The sight of it steeled Sarah. She had been on the point of dismissing Miss Yardley as one of the most vulgar young women she had ever met, but James's smug expression strengthened her backbone and made her determined to discover that Miss Yardley had hidden qualities which would make her eminently suited to being Dominic's wife.

'Have you visited any of the museums whilst you have been in London, Miss Yardley?' she asked, deftly turning the conversation away from the price of cloth.

'Why, yes, of course,' said Miss Yardley, happy to fall in with this new line of conversation. 'We have done most of them already. Haven't we, Pa?'

'That we have,' said her father, who had now finished his tea and was sitting with his legs out wide, straddling the elegant Hepplewhite chair as though it was a barrel-chested horse.

'But do you know, Miss Davenport, what I really long to see are the Nell Gwyn marbles. I do assure you they are all the rage. For although they are not on general view, it is possible to gain permission to see them. We are paying them a visit next week, are we not, Pa?'

Sarah worked hard to keep a straight face at this gaffe, a task made all the more difficult because she distinctly heard James splutter with laughter before quickly turning the laughter into a cough. But, despite Miss Yardley confusing Lord Elgin, a renowned traveller and collector of fine antiquities, with Nell Gwyn, the mistress of Charles II who, alas! had been dead for more than a hundred years, Sarah refused to admit that she had been wrong. Miss Yardley had made a mistake, she told herself. Anyone could make a mistake. And that was all.

And so she replied kindly, 'Ah! The *Elgin* marbles.' She corrected Miss Yardley without seeming to do so.

But Miss Yardley was having none of it. She had never taken kindly to being corrected—which was why she had remained ignorant on so many topics—and she was not going to be corrected now. It never once occurred to her that she might be wrong. Indeed, she did not care whether she was wrong or not. All she cared about was that she got her own way. So that she looked at Sarah haughtily and remarked, 'Oh, no, Miss Davenport. The *Nell Gwyn* marbles. Everyone has heard of the Nell Gwyn marbles. Isn't that so, Pa?'

'Aye, lass. Nell Gwyn. Just so.'

'Why, even my sister Charity has heard of Nell Gwyn, and she has not even seen the marbles, having just suffered her second confinement.'

Ladies' confinements were not generally mentioned in mixed society, but Sarah took up the subject nevertheless, hoping against hope that here she might find Miss Yardley's redeeming feature. 'She is well, I hope?'

'Oh, yes. Charity is always well. Though why she must always be having children is beyond me, I'm sure. Nasty, bawling things.'

Here her father unexpectedly chimed in. 'Nowt wrong wi' t'little 'uns. 'Appen you should be thinking of a few yoursen.'

Miss Yardley shuddered. 'They do nothing but cry until they are fully five years old,' she declared.

Sarah gave an inward sigh but made no attempt to put her right. She knew that Miss Yardley was not interested in children. She also knew that Miss Yardley did not want to know at what age children generally stopped crying.

No matter how unwillingly, Sarah had to admit that Miss Yardley was indeed both ignorant and vulgar.

She had to admit defeat.

*　　　*　　　*

'So, shall we give Miss Yardley and Dominic our blessing, Sarah?' It was an hour later. Miss Yardley and her father had departed, and James was strolling with Sarah through the elegant gardens that lay behind Randall House.

Sarah could not resist a gurgle of laughter as she recalled the disastrous afternoon. 'Poor Dominic! How could he have been so deceived?'

'Miss Yardley has a very pretty face and very pretty manners,' said James. 'She is well dressed and has an air of elegance. She is lively and talkative and, when she feels it is worth her while, she knows how to please. Add to that the fact that Dom has always been willing to believe the best of people, and it isn't difficult to see why he was so taken in.'

'Even so . . .'

James nodded. 'Even so, a marriage with Miss Yardley would have proved disastrous. Because Miss Yardley is indeed beneath him, and sooner or later Dom would have discovered it for himself. And if that had happened *after* their marriage, rather than before, it would have made him miserable.'

Sarah stopped. James stopped, too. She had been determined to discover that Miss Yardley was a lovely young woman but she had found quite the opposite. She had to admit that James was right. Miss Yardley *was* beneath Dominic. Not just because she came from a lower position in life. Not just because her family had no connections. But because, as James had known all along, she was ignorant and vulgar.

'Do you remember when you apologized to me about the children? When you had seen for yourself what a difference it made to Fitzwilliam's character—being allowed to play?' she asked. 'Well, this time I am the one who has to apologize. You were right and I was wrong. Miss Yardley is as vulgar as you claimed. It would have been a disaster if Dominic had married her.'

James smiled. 'Yes. It would have been disastrous. I am a proud man, Sarah, and I wouldn't have wanted Dom to marry someone without connections, but if he had truly loved her then I would not have stood in his way. It was my father who instilled such a strong sense of pride in me, and told me from the earliest age that I must marry someone from an old family.'

'Did you not object?' asked Sarah curiously.

He shook his head. 'I have to say that when I was younger marriage did not interest me, so that I was happy to go along with my father. The only thing that interested me was going into the army. My father had been understanding about my ambition—it is not usual for elder sons to go into the army, but I had my heart set on it, and he did not stand in my way and so I was happy to go along with him on the subject of marriage. Indeed, he arranged my first marriage for me.'

Sarah caught her breath. She had often wondered about James's first marriage. 'Was it . . . was it happy?' she asked.

He frowned. 'In its way, I suppose. I barely saw Rosabelle. After marrying her I deposited her at the Grange, and then went off to the continent to fight against Napoleon's armies. She went her way and I went mine. And that, I thought—not having anything to compare it to—was a happy marriage. So that when she died, and when I returned from the army, and when I realized I must marry again—it was either that or be pursued by a host of unmarried young ladies and their matchmaking mamas until I was in my dotage!—I decided to make another marriage of the same kind. I looked for a meek and quiet young lady who would not interfere with my life in any way.'

'And found her in the person of Miss Leatherhead?' asked Sarah, remembering the rumours that had been circulating in the village.

James gave a wry smile. 'And found her in the person of Miss Leatherhead,' he agreed. 'And I was all set to propose to her—until you came into my life. Telling me what I could and couldn't do. Making me think about you. Making me care about you. And making me realize that marriage had more to offer than meekness and obedience!'

'Poor Miss Leatherhead,' murmured Sarah.

James smiled. 'No. Not poor Miss Leatherhead. She is by now betrothed to Lord Brancaster—a young man who adores her, as she adores him.'

'Theirs at least is a suitable match,' Sarah teased.

'And so is ours,' smiled James. 'I didn't *want* to fall in love with a governess. I resisted it for a long time. But when it happened; when your absence forced me to acknowledge it . . .'

'Yes, James?' asked Sarah softly.

'When it happened I didn't care any more. Because once it had happened it didn't matter. I would have married you even if you'd been a scullery maid.'

Sarah nodded. 'I know that now. I think I would have known it at the time if I'd stopped to think about it, but you took me by surprise and I was already confused: so much had happened in such a short space of time.'

He nodded, understanding.

'Who was it who told you about Miss Yardley?' he asked curiously. 'Was it Dominic?'

Sarah shook her head. 'He mentioned Miss Yardley a few times in passing, but it was Mrs Smith who told me the whole story. That's what made me think you wouldn't have proposed to me if I'd still been a governess. I thought your only objection to her was her rank, instead of realizing your objection was founded on her personality as well. Do you forgive me for doubting you?'

'Only if you forgive me for having been a blind and arrogant fool, and taking far too long to see that I loved you, when I should have known at once.'

He bent his dark head and kissed her softly on the lips.

'I'm glad you're not angry with me any more,' she said, as his mouth finally left hers.

'I've never been angry with you.'

She gave a wry smile. 'Yes, you have, You were so angry with me for doubting you that you didn't come to see me in Bath.'

'You made it quite clear you didn't want to see me,' he returned.

'I waited for you to call every day,' she contradicted him. 'You didn't come. I couldn't think why. Were you really so angry that you would have been content to never see me again?'

He turned towards her with a frown. 'I called on you as soon as I had attended to all the necessary formalities, but I was told that you were "not at home". When I said I would call later—thinking that you were "not at home" because you were resting after your ordeal—I was told you would not be "at home" then either.'

'But I never gave instructions . . .' began Sarah, puzzled.

'No one else would have the necessary authority to—'

'Nicholas,' Sarah cut across him.

'Your brother?'

She gave a sigh. 'When I first started at the Grange, I sent him a number of letters which were . . . uncomplimentary,' she said ruefully. 'I told him you were—'

'Rude? Arrogant? High-handed?' asked James with a smile.

Sarah gave an answering smile of her own. 'Yes,' she admitted. 'Although I later told him that I had been wrong he wouldn't believe it. He persisted in seeing you as some kind of monster who had made his sister's life a misery. I should have guessed what he had done.'

'And I thought you were refusing to see me because the change in your fortunes had changed *you*,' said James, pulling Sarah's hand through his arm and walking on with her. 'But there is one thing I still don't understand,' he said thoughtfully. 'Why did you go to the cottage with Haversage in the first place? You knew he was up to something, or you wouldn't have sent me the note. So why did you agree to go with him?'

Briefly, Sarah explained about Lucy's hair, mentioning also that, at her suggestion, Lady

Templeton had seen to Nelly's dismissal for aiding and abetting Mr Haversage. As he listened to the story unfold James's grip on Sarah's hand tightened, as if he was determined to make sure that nothing ever threatened her again.

'I only hoped that you would understand the note,' she finished.

'I would have needed to have been a genius to understand it. But as soon as I read it I knew something was wrong.' He paused. 'I still can't decide whether it was brave or foolish of you to go with Haversage alone.'

'I knew I wouldn't be alone for long.'

'You never doubted that I'd come?'

She shook her head. 'Never. I trusted in you completely.'

He turned to face her. 'Those are some of the best words I have ever heard. There are only three words I'd like to hear more.' He turned to face her, his black eyes looking directly into her own and sending shivers of awareness down her spine. 'I love you, Sarah, but I need to know if my feelings are returned.'

'Oh, yes, James,' she said, smiling up at him. 'They are. I love you. With all my heart.'

He took her hands. 'I asked you once before to marry me. I'm asking you again now. Sarah, will you be my wife?'

'Oh, yes, James.'

And the kiss that followed was sweeter than

the one before.

It was broken off only when one of the gardeners appeared, trundling a wheelbarrow in front of him, at the end of the path.

'Although it might be unfair to Susannah,' said Sarah teasingly. 'I had just arranged with Lady Templeton that Susannah should be my replacement as Lucy's governess. It seems she won't be needed after all.'

'I think we'll appoint her,' said James. 'Lucy will need a governess—especially whilst we are on our honeymoon. We'll go to Paris. Now that the war is over, there's so much I want to show you.'

'And so much I want to see. And who knows,' she added thoughtfully, 'if Susannah spends the winter at the Grange . . .'

'Matchmaking, Sarah?' asked James with a smile. 'Who knows, you may be right? I think Dom and Susannah might suit very well. But not as well as us,' he added with a smile.

'Even though I turned your life upside down?' she teased him.

'*Because* you turned my life upside down,' he laughed. 'Because you taught me so much about life. And about the children. And the more I saw you with them, the more I longed to give you children of your own!'

'Wasn't that very improper?' Sarah teased him, giving him a sideways glance.

'Most improper,' he agreed with a wicked smile. 'But also, most enjoyable.' He put his finger under her chin and turned her face up so that her eyes met his own. 'You've taught me so much, Sarah. But, once I've made you my wife, there is so much I want to teach you.'

He kissed her again, softly at first, his lips barely grazing hers. Then slowly, tantalizingly, he forced her lips apart.

Her arms slid up to his muscular chest and twined themselves around his neck as his tongue explored her mouth, awakening new desires that thrilled her to her very core.

And when at last he pulled away she said, with a look that roused every masculine instinct in his body, 'If all the lessons are as enjoyable as that one, I can't wait to begin.'

We hope you have enjoyed this Large Print book. Other Chivers Press or Thorndike Press Large Print books are available at your library or directly from the publishers.

For more information about current and forthcoming titles, please call or write, without obligation, to:

Chivers Press Limited
Windsor Bridge Road
Bath BA2 3AX
England
Tel. (01225) 335336

OR

Thorndike Press
295 Kennedy Memorial Drive
Waterville
Maine 04901
USA

All our Large Print titles are designed for easy reading, and all our books are made to last.